Anno-Domini

The Christ Parable

By
Graham Manning

Strategic Book Publishing and Rights Co.

Strategic Book Publishing and Rights Co.
12620 FM 1960, Suite A4-507
Houston, TX 77065
www.sbpra.com

ISBN: 978-1-62516-047-8

Book Design: Suzanne Kelly

NO ONE KNOWS ABOUT THE DAY OR HOUR, NOT
EVEN THE ANGELS IN HEAVEN, NOR THE SON, BUT
ONLY THE FATHER.

MATTHEW 24:36

PROLOGUE

The silence of the crowd overhung with an aura of reverence, as the Pope gave the closing speech to his Christmas message. *"When the Son of God comes, will he still find faith on the earth? He will come suddenly, and the world will not be ready."*

"He will come in judgement for which man shall find himself unprepared, he will come to establish his kingdom in the world, and he will come in glory having defeated and annihilated the enemies of God the Father." (Luke 18:8)

The message went beyond the principle doctrine of the Vatican; this mandate was to consolidate the church's message to all nations, a manifestation of divine truth. The significance of the approaching days of the new millennium stirred within the hearts, hope and faith, as the gathering just looked above, their lips moving in silent prayer.

Alexandra Lombardi was the Pope's private secretary; an affable and quick-witted man, who was devoted to the ceremonial and administrative requirements of his job. Never far from the pontiff's side, meticulous and thorough, he missed nothing. He would oversee all aspects of the papal security on every major event in the calendar of the Pope's duties and travel commitments.

He watched as the Pope wished the pilgrims "Happy Christmas" in many different languages drawing delighted cheers from the large gathering. He was pleased with himself as everything had gone well, yet it was never far from his mind how that unassuming face in the crowd could be the one who makes an attempt on his Holiness's life.

Monsignor Gerard P Raffin rushed towards the private secretary gripping him by the forearm. Alexandra Lombardi turned quickly as he studied the startled yet familiar face.

"Monsignor Raffin, what is it – are you alright?" The grip on his forearm grew tighter and he noticed the Monsignor's hand was shaking and covered in blood. "It has begun; we do not have much time." The words stammering from his mouth, and the fear in his eyes were almost overwhelming. "They... they have both been killed." For a moment he bowed his head as he paused, "Slaughtered, torn to pieces, it has begun, God help us."

The two cardinals had preferred to travel by night, driving from Santa Fe, approximately forty miles northwest towards Los Alamos.

There had been no urgency along the journey to hold any conversation as the two men drove on in silence, instead isolated within the complexities of their thoughts. Although highly trained and fully aware of their purpose, they could not help but dwell within their fear and expectation of what lay ahead.

The car pulled into an isolated gas station, and for a moment waited as the elderly attendant shuffled across towards them. He pulled a rag from inside his overalls running it along the windscreen, before standing back as he studied the two men with a bemused curiosity. "What will it be padre?" he asked, his voice wheezing as he chewed on the butt of the cigar wedged tight against the corner of his mouth.

"Fill it up please," replied the elder of the two cardinals as he slowly began climbing out of the car while his younger companion remained in the passenger seat. "If you're lookin fer the John padre just head on out back and follow the sound of the flies puking up." The younger cardinal turned, looking over at the attendant who began to cackle loudly as he spluttered his cigar butt across the bonnet. "Sorry! Padre, I guess I don't see many folks round here much. It kinda changes a guy's perspective on humour an all."

They watched as he picked up the cigar butt and placed it in the corner of his mouth, biting down on it with one of the remaining teeth he still had.

"What brings you to the hill padre?" asked the attendant as he pushed the nozzle into the fuel flap. "The hill," replied the cardinal frowning. "Yeah the town site," said the attendant.

"This town used ta mean sumthin once," he went on, his eyes narrowing into two black slits across his haggard face. "Back in the day it had purpose, this shit piece of dirt created sumthin great." They watched as the attendant again began to cackle loudly. "Blew the shit out of them Jap bastards!" he continued, "and it was all done here, yeah the big bomb was made right here on the hill." The two cardinals watched in silence as the attendant continued cackling now wide-eyed in seemingly inane bursts.

He inserted the nozzle back in the fuel pump still grinning, as he continued to observe the cardinals with an unnerving scrutiny that was forced upon them with obvious intent.

The elder cardinal climbed back in the car and slammed the door shut. "Keep the change," he said, unable to hide the obvious disdain in his voice, as he handed a twenty dollar bill to the attendant who slowly crumpled it in his hand. "Would you be heading up towards the Calvary Chapel on the north road?" They looked upon him curiously as he asked the question, as if he already knew the answer.

"Yes that is right," replied the elderly cardinal. All of a sudden there was an uneasiness that seemed to move through him, like the pulling of a cold chain of dread, that although he felt he had to contain, the probing glare of the attendant seemed to peel away at his thoughts, as if psychologically his inward revelations were rendered naked before this man.

The attendant gave a broad smile, "Don't thinks the padre's home tonight." His burst of laughter seemed to pierce the night stillness as the two cardinals drove off.

He watched as the plume of dust from the departing car seemed to cling upon the darkness before him, shuffling against the void above. His hand still clenching the twenty-dollar bill before his fingers slowly opened.

"Seek and you shall find," he said grinning, as the twenty in his hand burst into flames. He turned, walking back towards the gas station. His shape suddenly began to shimmer and distort, the bone and cartilage in his body began to stretch and break as he changed back to what he really was. He passed solitarily, across towards the attendant, whom he had killed earlier. The crumpled body and terrified open-eyed glare bore the slither of his murderer's shadow that was cast, as if it was pulled across his face, like a shimmering veil. He turned, walking out towards the desert.

The silence within the car, combined with the tension felt by the two cardinals, caused the vehicle to swerve along the narrow north road as they headed towards the Calvary Chapel. The apex of the church stood solemn against the darkness as the overall shape seemed to slope eerily upon the hill, an uneven row of multicoloured bulbs dangled across the entrance. The elder cardinal could not help thinking it resembled some unconventional lustrous parody of what it was meant to stand for, almost like the entrance of a house of ill repute. He frowned at the absurdity of his thoughts.

The car came to a stop upon a small grass verge that dipped along the path of the entrance.

The younger cardinal pulled a semi-automatic handgun from within a well-concealed shoulder holster. "I have a feeling that will not be necessary," said his companion grimly as he climbed from the car studying the outline of the building. They walked towards the small arched entrance and for a moment the silence seemed to throb in the warm night air.

The elder cardinal carefully placed his hand against the door and pushed it inwards.

Sprinkles of light flickered against the rough wooden surface, stirring a row of burning candles as it moved across the immediate darkness from within. His younger colleague gripped the gun tightly against his chest in a heightened anticipation he could not hide, his eyes moving nervously around the interior.

For a moment they stood within the concaved entrance listening as if suspended within the silence before slowly walking inwards.

They noticed for the first time how small the interior actually was and the dim glow of the candles only perpetuated this. A large oval window hung upon the centre wall at the front of the church, high enough to capture what fragments of moonlight still remained in the dark sky, as the clouds shifted and clung together choking away what little light remained.

"Wait," said the elder cardinal gripping his colleagues arm. He looked towards the small altar before turning away; a look of despair fell across his face as he slowly closed his eyes, "We are too late." Father Emanuel Hernandez lay naked sprawled across the altar; a silver-coloured ornate crucifix had been forced through his forehead almost pinning him to the surface. His arms were raised, hands outstretched claw-like rigid, as if the corpse had been entombed by the same lingering terror he had encountered before his death.

They stood in silence for a moment unable to move, the only sound was the soft dripping of blood that poured from the dead priest across his face and shoulders, along the altar and onto the floor.

The elder cardinal walked towards the body, he studied the words that had been torn across the dead man's chest ANNO DOMINI (in the year of our Lord Jesus Christ). It had been the same as the others. He slowly made the sign of the cross. He was the ninth priest to have been killed in as many hours and the clock was still ticking.

ONE

His eyes blinked as the stirring of the curtains distracted him from his thoughts, frowning, looking towards the window as the dull winter daylight poured across the floor near to where he sat.

He moved slowly across the room towards the window where he would remain for some time just observing.

He observed the outside world, the slow movement of the trees, the breeze weaving across the long grass in slight flurries like ripples on water. The soft screams and laughter of children trickled off the walls in faint echoes, as they played beyond the hospital's boundaries, only to dwindle and fade like the daylight hours around him.

His imagination took him down the path, struggling to open the large iron gates, he watched himself stroke the bark of a tree, running his fingers along a drooping branch caressing the moist leaves, feeling their dampness across the palms of his hands.

He was observing life, his life, the everyday things in the world we are given freely, the simple things granted by God himself.

He marvelled at the clarity of his imagination as he looked upon himself as he walked upon the world. For a time he was free to walk away from the restraints his physical burdens had placed upon him.

Yet there were flickers of images and thoughts that lay distant beyond his understanding, images and thoughts that were not just his, but of those around him.

This was something that snatched him back towards what was real, and this clarity of mind was not to be marvelled at, instead it terrified him.

There was a slight tremble as his hand folded around the silver crucifix that hung loosely around his buttoned-up shirt. He had finally stopped asking why? Why he had been left like this? He still would look back, back to when he was a child, back before the accident.

Gabriel Salmach had been twelve years old when the car being driven by his father had been forced off the road killing both his parents. The crash would leave him severely paralysed for the rest of his life. WHY? This word, which he had caressed and sculpted within his mind many times, was something he grew to hate. The very sound of it made the contents in his stomach want to rush out through his mouth and spew out upon such an unfair world.

He would remember his mother wrapping the collars of his coat around his neck and tucking the knot of the red scarf into his jumper kissing him on the forehead, as she played with his fringe. The snow had fallen hard that day. "Say goodbye Gabriel," she said clutching his hand, as they stood outside the house which had been their home for the past two years. The demands of his father's job had forced them to move closer to London. He still missed his father, he was close to his mother yet there had been a bond that they had shared. It was almost as if the nurturing had been left unfinished between father and son, something had been broken and would remain unfixed.

His father had worked for the British government. His work had taken him all over the world; he had worked for a time in Bahrain, then Nairobi, and for a couple of years in the Middle East. Born in Egypt at the start of the Second World War, Nebi Salmach was forced to grow up very quickly. Witnessing his own father get his throat slit over a gambling debt, and left to bleed to death outside a backstreet whorehouse.

That was situated on the bad side of the city of Cairo. Nebi had watched the men laughing as his father lay dying. He watched as they urinated on him, he did not cry, even though he was powerless to do anything, as he himself would have almost certainly been killed.

All he could do was watch, watch and remember their laughing faces. Their faces would remain with him for some time.

It would be six years until he had found the last of the men and killed him. The man had pleaded the most, he begged and screamed, but the boy, then eighteen, did not hesitate, he just slit his throat slower. The men had all died the same way they had killed his father, except he did not urinate on them, he was not an animal, he had pride and even though he knew it was wrong, he enjoyed the revenge, it felt good, so good he could almost taste it, the one thing that surprised him was how easy he found it was to kill.

Life had driven a spear through his heart at a young age, somehow dispelling his innocence and compassion, leaving him as cold as a midnight gravestone.

Nebi knew he would have to get out of the city and that chance came when his friend had fled Egypt due to a falling out with a local gangster boss. Nebi's friend had got a girl pregnant; no big deal except it was the gangster boss's wife. And a price had been put on his testicles literally.

They found work in South Africa after crossing the Sudan and heading south towards Kenya and Nairobi, working as gun-runners with a group of mercenaries.

They bought guns from Dutch traders where the mercenaries sold them to the Mau Mau who were an anti-white terrorist society, and who in turn used them to kill white settlers.

For a while Nebi and his friend stayed on the outskirts of the Kikuyu tribal reserve in the white highlands, which was under Mau Mau control. They witnessed the atrocities the Mau Mau was capable of in their aim at ending colonial rule. Inoffensive civilians were systematically butchered and beaten to death; this brutish indifference bordered on animalistic barbarism, as the brains of human victims were eaten, babies killed and battered, slaughtered like stale meat in front of their mothers. These people seemed beyond human. Not an ideal way to make a living, as Nebi would find out when a particular deal went wrong and his friend was killed by the Mau Mau. He was tortured and cut to pieces before his body was burned. Many of the guns

3

did not work; they had been double-crossed by the Dutch, and many more paid with their lives. He had barely escaped with his own life escaping across the highlands towards the Aberdare Mountains.

Nebi had come across a farmhouse which had been almost burned down except for a portion of the rear that had remained intact. He found three bodies, one of whom was a child that was dead along with the woman, the man was barely conscious but he was alive. A single Mau Mau terrorist remained and was torching the farmhouse when Nebi overpowered and killed him, before he died the terrorist kept repeating the word "Shaitan" pointing towards the farmhouse. He carried the semi-conscious man for almost a day and a half until they were found by Samburu tribal trackers, who had been organised to hunt the terrorists.

They were taken to southern Nairobi; to a British outpost where they were fed and Nebi had learned as he was interrogated by security forces from Kenya that the man whose life he had saved was a British diplomat. The man was treated for his wounds, which were quite severe, but he would live. His name was Jonathan Frazier the son of Sir Reginald Frazier a member of parliament and head of MI6. Nebi had questioned the meaning of the word "Shaitan" and was stunned at the trackers' response, it meant Devil.

Jonathan Frazier had lived in Kenya for two years before the unrest between blacks and whites. Nebi had explained how he had come across the farmhouse which had been set on fire, and was almost burned down to the ground, and how he had been looking for food, when he had found him unconscious and barely alive.

He did not mention the wife and child, that although dead and judging by the injuries they had suffered, death had not been quick.

"I guess I owe you my life," said the diplomat, his left arm had been badly burned which would leave a severe scar running from the shoulder down towards the back of the hand. The extent of the burns would cause both the index and forefinger to be fused together.

"We were both lucky to come out of this alive," he paused for a moment. "I am sorry about your family," continued Nebi, reaching into a bowl and scooping up the cool water soaking his face.

"You're not African," said the diplomat.

"No, I have travelled from Egypt down the Nile and across the Sudan with a friend, we were looking for work," said Nebi.

"What kind of work?" asked the diplomat, as he studied the young Egyptian curiously.

"I suppose that would depend on who is paying, and what they are paying," replied Nebi, running the water through his hair.

"My father could use somebody like you. I am travelling to Morocco to meet with him in Marrakesh. He has flown there from England; we leave the day after tomorrow, after I bury my wife and child." The diplomat for a moment, seemed lost in his words, yet Nebi could sense indifference in his tone as if some other primary importance occupied his thoughts other than the death of his family. Jonathan Frazier averted from Nebi's gaze as he slowly turned and left the room and revealed more than he wanted to.

* * *

The whirring of the ceiling fan cut through the silence as the man in the white suit sat in the corner of the police commissionaire's office. The brim of his panama hat was turned down, sending a swooping shadow falling across his face.

"I believe you are looking for work?" asked the man.

"Yes that is right," said Nebi as he slowly walked over to the wicker chair and sat in it. A mixture of suspicion and curiosity seemed constrained by his demeanour that only made his reservations and fear more obvious.

"Allow me to introduce myself, I am Sir Reginald Frazier, and I am in charge of an organisation based in London that is responsible for gathering intelligence outside Britain."

"What is that to do with me?" asked Nebi curiously.

"Well, there are certain individuals who are scattered around the world, who we see as a threat to our national security," he paused for a moment leaning backwards. "And to put it bluntly," he continued, "they need to be removed."

"I took the liberty of running a check against your background; you were born in Giza, which is west of Cairo I believe, and your mother still lives there. But your father… your father is no longer alive, he had the misfortune to have his throat slit outside a house of ill repute in Cairo a number of years ago; the perpetrators were never caught or likely to be, is that not right Nebi?" Sir Reginald leaned forward his dark eyes narrowing as he studied him.

"Yes that's right, they are all dead," replied Nebi. "I killed them."

"Yes you did. Slit their throats, all of them, a fitting sort of poetic retribution if I may say." Sir Reginald tipped the bottle by his side, and poured the whisky, filling a quarter of the crystal glass and drank it in one.

"I killed them because they deserved it," said Nebi. "I killed them in the memory of my father. They killed him like an animal so they died like animals."

"Yes quite," replied Sir Reginald. "But remember Mr Salmach, if everyone on this planet was to be killed because they deserved it in one way or another, there would not be enough people left to fill this room, you see, Mr Salmach," he continued, "we kill out of necessity."

"I leave for England tomorrow, do you have a passport?"

"Yes," replied Nebi.

Sir Reginald rose from his chair. "I will be in the hotel lobby across the street at 6. in the morning, if you are there, I take it you would like to work for me. Good day Mr Salmach."

Nebi rose from his chair, and watched Sir Reginald walk towards the door. "Oh, I almost forgot, thank you for saving my son's life."

TWO

L ondon seemed like another planet to the young Egyptian boy; the large bustling metropolis thudded and pulsated, vibrating like the heartbeat of the world itself.

He seemingly walked around the city in a daze; the large buildings stood oppressive and harsh against the dull skyline, yet strangely majestic and beautiful.

He would walk among the people as if invisible, he was a number, a digit, and he was nothing.

He was sent to a "safe house" above a rare bookshop, situated about a mile from Westminster Bridge Road, where the intelligence service was based. For the first few days he heard nothing, on the third day an envelope was pushed under his door, on opening it he found some money with a note asking him to go to the entrance of St Paul's Cathedral.

Nebi stood before the great Anglican cathedral as he marvelled at the huge Portland stone structure. Christopher Wren's wondrous monument had been built in a late Renaissance style representing England's "sobering" baroque, astounding today as when it had been constructed in the early seventeenth century (it was constructed betweeb 1675–1710) replacing its predecessor that had succumbed to the great fire of London. He stared for a moment upon the cross at the summit as if it stirred the movement of the clouds above. A great inclination befell him of the sudden need to touch the building, as if its inspiration and redemption would befall him, cleanse him of all sin he had committed, so that he may turn and face the world like some reborn child allowed to start again in a world that would be "kinder" to him. His eyes fell upon the large dome he knew had been inspired by St Peter's Basilica in Rome; it was something he had learned in school, and could not help feeling a stirring within as he stood before this testament to the Lord God. He looked away from the cross above, closing his eyes, as his motive for coming here was not to pray, and not to seek redemption.

He waited by the great west door for about twenty minutes, just watching the passers-by going about their early morning business. A group of schoolchildren were escorted in line by their teacher, as they were halted towards the entrance. He watched the teacher slowly walk down the line tapping each pupil's head as they were slowly counted and ticked off the register.

The loud cheers from the pupils as the teacher announced they would be entering the cathedral in a couple of minutes, caused a spray of pigeons to fly out from the clock tower, the flapping wings seemed to rasp against the crisp morning air as if in slow motion as they slowly dispersed across the sky.

Nebi was approached by a tall smartly dressed man in a dark pinstriped suit; his hair was slicked back, seemingly cut and combed with meticulous precision. His eyes were covered by dark glasses, and there was a grace and confidence as he moved.

"Good morning, Mr Salmach, my name is Phillip Rackman. I work for Sir Reginald Frazier; I trust you had a good flight? And the dwellings we have provided for you are adequate?"

His features were stern and harsh. He looked like a man who had embodied every emotion the world could bestow upon a human. Rackman stood with his hands crossed just observing Nebi.

"Yes… they are adequate," replied Nebi.

"It's magnificent, would you not agree?" said Rackman. Nebi looked on confused. "Why the cathedral, of course?" he continued, as he gestured for Nebi to walk alongside him. "Yes it is beautiful," replied Nebi.

"Took a bit of a bashing during the war, yet there was nothing too serious thankfully." They walked along the west side of the cathedral.

"What am I to do?" asked Nebi.

"As Sir Reginald briefly explained, there are certain individuals and organisations throughout the world and in this very country." For a moment he paused, stopping as he looked upon the cathedral. "Who are dangerous to our way of life, we are at war Mr Salmach," he continued. "A silent war, yet there are many casualties, many casualties indeed."

Rackman reached inside his jacket pulling out a brown envelope and slowly handed it to Nebi. "Inside this envelope there is five hundred pounds, you will receive the same amount when the assignment is completed. Also, there is a photo of a man and some details of who this man is, by this time next week he is taking a trip to Russia." Again he paused looking around, "We don't want him to make that trip do you understand, Mr Salmach?"

Nebi studied the photo for a moment. "Why me?" he asked, "I mean surely you have your own people?"

"Yes that is true, Mr Salmach. We do have our own people, but how can I say? There is a certain inconspicuousness you being a foreign national and an unknown to the group this man is connected to." There was irreverence in the remark that Nebi felt was masked by a smile yet bore the inversion of a frown.

"Many of our people's lives depend on this, Mr Salmach. People who are working undercover in the 'field' who are connected to this man, and who this man is about to betray."

"You will need this, Mr Salmach." Rackman grabbed Nebi's forearm, and ushered him towards a doorway, he looked around before passing him a sealed package. "This is a single-action pistol, with a single-stack magazine, which holds nine rounds; the gun is loaded and also untraceable. There is also a detachable silencer, which you will find very helpful." For a moment Rackman watched as Nebi ran his hand across the package, feeling the contours of the weapon before carefully placing it inside his breast pocket.

"I feel this concludes our business." Rackman stood as if carved from the gloom in the dull stone archway, as bloodless and cold as the stone itself.

"Good luck Mr Salmach."

Nebi watched Rackman walk away; disappearing within a small throng of people, an omnipresence hung within the air long after this man had gone, like a lingering spectre harbouring some great future dread.

THREE

VATICAN CITY

The Vatican City seemed unusually silent as the oncoming dusk stirred and moved the diminishing shadows that fell upon the dying light of day. An uneasy stillness penetrated the twilight gloom that oozed across St Peter's square willowing and caressing the pillars of the Apostolic Palace. It was almost as if the slow movement bore the ghosts of the great Renaissance painters that lingered within the churches and chapels; they were engraved upon the architecture beyond the frescoed walls and ceilings that bore the essence of their beings and the still air of their once great presence.

The Apostolic Palace is a company of buildings which includes the papal apartments, some of the Catholic Church's government offices, a handful of chapels, and the "Musei Vaticani" Vatican museum. Also the Vatican library, Bibliotheca Apostolica Vaticana. The library is one of the oldest in the world housing over seventy-five thousand manuscripts, and contains one of the most significant collections of historical texts. This had been where the first murder took place. In all there are over one thousand rooms, with the most famous being Raphael's rooms, and of course, the "Cappela Sistina" or Sistine Chapel. This was where the second priest was found.

The Sistine Chapel is a high rectangular brick building, with an exterior unadorned by architectural or decorative details; this is common in many Medieval and Renaissance churches in Italy. There is no exterior façade or processional doorways, as the ingress of the building has always been from internal rooms within the Papal Palace. The exterior can be seen only from nearby windows and light-wells from inside.

The internal spaces are divided into three stories, of which the lowest is huge, initiating a robustly spacious vaulted basement, where there are several utilitarian windows more for the practical use, rather than their aesthetic value, pertaining to the obvious beauty surrounding the exterior court.

The vaulted ceiling rises to just less than 21 metres, the building had six tall arched windows down each side, and two at the other end. Many of these have now been blocked, but the chapel is still accessible. An open projecting gangway encircles the building supported by an arcade that seems to spring from the walls. The gangway had been roofed, as it fed a continual source of water that leaked upon the vault of the chapel.

The ceiling of the chapel is a concave barrel-like vault that springs from a course that encircles the walls in line at the level of the window arches. This vault is situated crosswise by smaller vaults, dividing the ceiling at its lowest level into large overhanging pendentives rising between each window into triangular sections.

Lower parts of the walls are decorated in frescoed wall hangings of silver and gold, where the centre depicts the life of Moses and the life of Christ.

The ceilings commissioned by Pope Julius II and painted by Michaelangelo have a series of nine paintings showing God's creation of the world, God's relationship with mankind, and the subsequent fall from God's grace by man. Upon the pendentives that support the vault, are biblical paintings of both men and women who prophesied God would send back his son for the salvation of mankind.

There had been a major reshuffle of the Papal staff and Monsignor Gerard P Raffin had been promoted to one of the most important posts in the Vatican, the new prefect of the congregation of bishops. At almost six feet four, his personality differed from the more austere and sombre personnel of that within the church. He would smile broadly and willingly grasp a stranger's hand, making all that encountered him appear on a level "playing field" of mental equality, his understanding eased what dispositions, or uncertainties may lurk within the individual, when met by such a "high-ranking" Vatican official. Even though his mind was superior to most and his nature aroused only meaningfulness and good, he could be extremely manipulative without being obvious. He had the power to nominate, with the Pope's approval, new bishops from anywhere in the world.

Monsignor Raffin was Canadian, born in Edmonton in southwest Canada at the foot of the Great Slave Lake. He was a young sixty-three, with a fresh outlook; he understood the importance of his position having joined the priesthood in Calgary when he was eighteen.

The Vatican was, in a way, becoming restructured; it could be considered to be "moving with the times", as sixteen out of twenty-two offices are now headed by foreigners. Monsignor Raffin headed the congregation of cardinals; this was one arm of the Vatican that was to assist the sovereign pontiff in the administration of the affairs of the church. Numerous religious representatives from all over the world had recently travelled to Rome at the Vatican's request.

The most inward concern by the Vatican had been the recent slaughter of the two priests who were literally torn to pieces. This had not been made public, one had been found in the Vatican library pinned to the floor, his head had been removed, the other hanging from the ceiling beside the wall by the altar of the Sistine Chapel, he was left dangling naked opposite Michelangelo's *The Last Judgement* a depiction of the second coming of Christ and the Apocalypse. The blood of the priest had sprayed across the wall, as the severity of his wounds had left parts of his body in pieces, it had been clear their deaths had been at the hands of something that seemed inhuman.

Born from absolute religious purity they had been "chosen", monitored from birth and monitored everyday of their lives. Groomed from the day they had been born to line the path of Christ as a mortal, as he had been born onto the flesh of man. The priests had been scattered across the world only coming together on the final remaining days of the century. Only when the Christ was found and revealed, the gathering would take place upon the eve of the new millennium. Monsignor Raffin and the company of cardinals had anticipated these recent events, anticipating the oncoming evil, eleven priests had been chosen by man, the twelfth would be brought forth by the biblical messianic prophecy.

There had been many different faiths and religions brought together by the Curia, the Vatican's administrative body.

This gathering of religious scholars and leaders from these countries had been brought together by a newly formed world congress, many in this gathering whose neighbours had been their great enemies, stood side by side. Peace talks in the Middle East had been set into motion by this "outside order" and concessions and placations were not an option, as rumours had been rife of this "peace agreement" as to what concessions had been made to facilitate it by this world government.

One such concession that was met with hostility was that Islamic people would share in the new Jewish temple rebuilt upon the mount in Jerusalem, a temple of worship, and a place of self-atonement for the Jewish people's sin. Yet, this act of re-establishing a ritual of sacrifice was also considered a rejection of Christ. Crucifixion was seen as the ultimate sacrifice for the Jewish people, as it is for all of mankind.

Monsignor Raffin had addressed this mass of religious dignitaries, but there was contempt and disbelief, for some the only importance was the hatred for each other and the self-preservation of their own lands and boundaries, and whom and what they worshipped. Their self-given right to spread their own teachings and philosophy however clearly inept, he could see they possessed greed and naivety, and they possessed spite and resentfulness. It was his anticipation of an obvious human trait that even people who appeared to have religious fortitude for their beliefs and sacrifices, could not see beyond their own delusions, and hatred for their fellow man, as they bare their differing creeds and confessions of faith and belief.

"Armageddon is no delusion ladies and gentlemen," said Monsignor Raffin as he walked to the forefront of the congregation. "The continuity of mankind could be the delusion in itself, are we to believe with such invalidating evidence by our own making within this 'nuclear age' that we…" he paused, pressing his fingers against his chest, "so deserve to reign within our self-deluded supremacy upon this planet?" He was looked upon in silence by the mass. "Armageddon is very real," he continued, walking around the gathering. "It is prophesised, the nuclear armed Muslim Antichrist will be attacked in the mountain region of the valley of Megiddo, Revelation 16: 16 this by armies of the north and east, will this bring about this anticipated Armageddon we so deserve? I do believe this Armageddon will be our own doing, but as the finality of such events unfolds it is we who will pay the price, at the hands of a far greater evil, other than man can do to man."

"Events are unfolding as we approach this coming millennium," he went on. "In a way we represent Heaven and Hell, good and evil, ladies and gentlemen, and let me tell you, this greater evil will prevail because we will allow it to. It flourishes within our greed and hatred." Again he paused, walking forward towards the congregation, before continuing, "It has been known that for over thirty years the Son of God has been living on this planet among us." There were gasps from the crowds.

"You… you have proof of this?" asked a somewhat startled English archbishop; there was incredulity in his stare, as he stepped forward shaking his head.

"From the day of his birth eleven priests were chosen to line the path of the return of the Son, in the coming days, they represent the Apostles of the Lord," replied Monsignor Raffin.

"I do not see what this signifies," said the archbishop raising his hands. Again the Monsignor stood in silence, "Most of these priests are dead, killed horrifically, murdered within hours of each other and within different countries across the world, and no one knew of their importance, no one knew of their significance, their existence outside the Vatican was known by no one. Two were recently found butchered within these very walls, and nothing has been released to the public."

There was a fervent chatter among the gathering. An Islamic imam stepped forward.

"Do you know by whom or why these murders were committed?" he asked folding his arms.

Monsignor Raffin scanned the expectant faces within the crowd. "Yes we do," he replied, raising his eyes slightly, "I would have thought that was obvious, it is mankind's personification of evil... the Devil."

Monsignor Raffin held up his hands at the expectant array of questions, before responding.

"He too walks the earth, and will stop at nothing in finding the Christ before he returns from flesh and blood to spiritual glory." The Monsignor for a moment smiled as he stared beyond the crowd. "Here in the midst of our naivety and doubt to what is real and happening before us, we have by our own hands created many hells upon the earth, and there are many devils among us, but believe me," he continued, his voice raising, "the hell that exists within our nightmares, and all our worst fears and content shall pour fourth upon us, and exist around us."

"Monsignor, if I may," an elderly Rabbi stepped forward. "If I may be frank," he continued, "you ask us to believe that the Christ, for whom some of the faith of Judaism has not a single official view on, and rejects his status as the Jewish Messiah, and the idea of this second coming." The Rabbi shrugged his shoulders, before continuing, "Surely his physical death failed to redeem the world."

"Monsignor," the Rabbi went on, "is it now time for another chance at a failed redemption of this world? Is this 'second coming' a compensation for an unfulfilled existence the first time around?"

"Rabbi, I respect your words, your views and beliefs, as I do all of you. There are many religions and faiths among us, but I believe we all pray and worship to whatever God we choose, to that 'higher being' we choose to worship. But on this night," he continued, "I pray that in the coming days and hours the one true God shall protect his son, from the evil that will rise among us, and if, as you say," he walked across towards the Rabbi, "I will pray that his existence will 'fulfil' the messianic prophecies this second time around." The Monsignor smiled at the Rabbi, placing a hand on his shoulder, but could not hide the concern in his eyes which in turn the Rabbi sensed.

"Do we know where he is?" asked the archbishop, not hiding the sardonic smile, whose intent was flung across towards the Monsignor. "Well we have people across all the major cities in the world, and I am afraid we have recently learned another priest has been killed before we could get to him, and that was in your country, and we have monitored many leading Satanists who in the last few days have headed there." The archbishop stood back in bewilderment, his expression bereft of sarcasm.

"Satanists," said the archbishop almost dismissively.

"Yes," replied the Monsignor. "Satanists. Devil worshippers, whatever you wish to call them. But I can assure you," he went on, "that they are very real and organised, and they too have spread through many cities and countries throughout the world, proliferating like a cancer. They too have been aware of the coming incarnation of Christ. And they will stop at nothing in their endeavours to destroy anything contrary in their belief of the coming of their master." Many of the congregation just looked at each other in silence. "You see," continued the Monsignor, "it is quite simple, if this is allowed, and on the slaying of the Christ, he shall walk the earth forever. Famine, war and devastation of our lands and eternal suffering shall be unleashed upon us for a thousand years, unlike anything we have ever known."

The Monsignor walked towards the forefront of the gathering, and for a moment he bowed his head in silence.

"If I appear worried ladies and gentlemen," he said raising his head up slowly, smiling, "let me assure you, it is because I am."

He paused again.

"On this night we must find a common ground, and we must join as one," he continued, "forge together in unity, first we must find the Christ, and also, he raised his forefinger, and find the location of the Gateway. The Middle East must find this unity, Israel and the countries of Islam must find this common ground." His eyes narrowed as he studied the congregation, before continuing, "Follow the true meaning of Islam, for submission and peace, that which this happening has been prophesised, and what is now happening amongst ourselves, and has happened in the past is now secondary."

The Islamic scholar stepped forward, "Monsignor you speak of peace within our lands, what guarantee, do we have, if we are to abide by this concession that other countries will follow? As you must understand, committing to this could leave us vulnerable."

"That is simple," he replied. "There is no choice, if you wish to survive."

Once again a silence washed over the gathering, stirring within the confines of their surroundings, until a slight muttering began to trickle through the crowd, as the elderly Rabbi stepped forward.

"Monsignor," he said as he slowly walked across the room easing him-self upon a small carved wooden chair that stood beside an elongated window, for a moment he just studied the younger man before him.

"My people are resolute," he said. "We have learned to be strong, as many times in our history we have been the victims, and watched our families perish, our homes destroyed, and our belongings and wealth relinquished between those who wished to eradicate us as a race. We will no longer be the victims, Monsignor that is our solemn promise to ourselves, and our ancestors. And we will survive when others have long perished, however!" he continued, "We are many things, and stupid is not one of them. Unfortunately!" The Rabbi slowly rose to his feet, "I feel the sincerity and truth in what you say to be real, it seems quite simple, the Son of God has been sent to protect and save us, not only from man's greatest enemy, he went on raising his arm pointing towards the gathering, which is each other, how foolish we must seem in the eyes of God, and at times how pathetic as a creation we have proved, when we are the givers of life and have the choice of love, yet our free will can only choose death and destruction as a given preference. I feel we must try to look beyond the smog of hatred and indifference, maybe what is happening is the culmination of our actions, now only our choices can save ourselves." The gathering just watched in silence as the Rabbi walked towards the door. He smiled, "I do this not out of naivety, I am aware of the theories surrounding these events, I do this out of necessity. We will set into motion the 'concessions' you speak of." He turned, facing the Monsignor, "We have faced many devils in our history, helping to destroy another one would be as you say Monsignor 'no big deal'," the Rabbi shrugged his shoulders with a wry smile, before turning and walking out.

"This Gateway," said the archbishop, "do we know of its whereabouts?"

"Well..." said the Monsignor, "it is thought the gate, like the Devil can manifest at any location, again!" he continued, raising his finger, "We are closely monitoring recent events in your country." The archbishop walked towards Monsignor Raffin holding his hands together as if in prayer as he pressed the forefingers against his mouth. "Forgive my scepticism, Monsignor, but I am sure I speak for everyone in this room, this 'story' this 'mysterious, world order' you speak of, I am sure you can prove these fantastic revelations, you share with us, again... forgive my suspicions," he went on, "but how do we know this is not some globalist agenda by the Vatican, to initiate an authoritarian world government, with an underlying motive for complete control, over both politics and finance?" The archbishop raised his arms, before continuing. "I am aware of the realms of fiction being stirred here, Monsignor, as I am sure we all are. Something like this would only evoke panic in the masses, stirring frenzy amongst fundamentalist Christians who are already concerned with the end-time emergence of the Antichrist."

There seemed to be an intense silence in the still air that hung upon the gathering. Monsignor Raffin walked forward, "I know what I am saying may seem vague or..." he turned to face the archbishop, "incredibly fictitious, but the Vatican's 'underlying motive' is its survival. I'm afraid it is as simple as that, what we do know of these manifestations is that they are brought about by the summoning of man."

"But what can be done?" asked the Islamic imam stepping forward.

"As I have said, we have representatives everywhere, we know from recent events and reports aforementioned," replied the Monsignor. "The present location is your country," he continued, pointing at the archbishop. "As to what can be done, well, first do not let your scepticism shroud what is very real and happening as we stand here now, second, we must unite our faiths and beliefs as one..." for a moment he paused, bowing his head as he tugged at the crucifix around his neck, "... and then hope."

FOUR

There was something about this city as dusk began to sweep across the streets of London. Its quaint shops and bistros full of life, young couples meeting and falling in love, holding hands in all-night cafés, laying out their dreams and hopes, laying out their lives and fears. Streets entwined like a million veins around this pumping heart of the world, there was a certain romanticism shrouded in its silence as night fell.

People mingled amidst the twilight hours, yielding secrets within their hearts and lives. The streets coupled with a thousand destinies and hidden sinister pasts, only broken by uncertain footsteps echoing in their comings and goings.

Olivia Hathaway had noticed the young foreign-looking boy for the past three nights, sitting at the same table just staring across the street. He could not have been much older than twenty, his pencil-thin moustache, which was carefully cut short running neatly across his top lip, gave him the unintentional look of a young Clarke Gable. His jet-black hair was swept back falling into a parting across his forehead just above his sharp brown eyes that had met hers more than once. He would drink three cups of coffee, smoking half a dozen cigarettes, before getting up to leave.

He was halfway through his second cup when Olivia, who had been a waitress at the small all-night café for about seven months, approached him.

"Are you ready for a refill sir?" she stood shaking the coffee pot, smiling.

For a moment he carefully studied the young woman, whose obvious beauty captivated him, as it had not been the first time he had noticed her.

"Ah I see! I am what you would call a creature of habit am I?"

"Well, I guess you pick these little things up in this job."

"Oh, and what little things would that be?" replied Nebi.

"Observing people, or more their habits," replied Olivia refilling Nebi's coffee cup.

"Erm... you mean observing like a spy? I thought that was illegal in this country."

"Well, that's true, but it depends on whom or what you are observing," she said smiling, blushing slightly.

Nebi smiled as he watched her walk back towards the counter.

He turned, looking out of the window and lit another cigarette, as he continued with his own observing. There was a casino across the street. He watched the various cars pull up along the road outside the casino entrance. He waited until the black Jaguar slowly drew up. The driver quickly emerged, as he shifted towards the rear left passenger door.

Nebi moved forward in his chair, peering through the window. James Hilary had been an agent for MI6 for several years, he had worked undercover in Syria in the Middle East, but for the past two years had been a double agent working for the KGB, the commission of state security in Russia. Nebi had been fully briefed. It was strongly rumoured he was part of a British spy ring, and this bubble of speculation had recently burst as the evidence became overwhelming through the infiltration of a government mole. Others were being investigated, and in the following weeks James Hilary was to fly to Moscow never to return to England, after giving up the names of hundreds of British agents scattered around the world in doing so signing their death warrants.

Hilary had been secretly investigated for several months by a secret organisation.

Within the British government known as the "core" he was the first high-profile agent to be marked.

James Hilary pulled a large cigar from inside his breast pocket as he emerged from the car; the driver quickly closed the door before reaching into his pocket for a lighter. He flicked the lighter, and the flame rose seemingly cutting through the darkness as the two men became etched against the faint glow.

The driver got back in the car and drove off. For a moment, Hilary puffed on the cigar before walking towards the casino entrance. Nebi watched as the two doormen acknowledged James Hilary knowingly as he walked in.

Nebi sipped the last of his coffee, got up and walked towards the counter.

"Do you live around here?" he asked Olivia, as she rinsed the last of a row of coffee cups, putting them upside down beside the sink turning the tap off.

"Do you work for the police?" she asked.

Nebi smiled, "No, I am just an interested customer who it so happens is attracted to one of this establishment's employees." Nebi leaned forward studying the name badge on her apron. "Olivia, you have a beautiful name. My name is Nebi."

"I am pleased to meet you, Nebi," she replied. "I live in Kensington with a girlfriend; we share a basement flat at the moment, it suits us both and it is cheaper, you don't look like a local," she went on.

"No I'm from Egypt," said Nebi. "I am over here studying."

"What may I ask?" replied Olivia.

"English!" he said. "How do you think I'm doing?" he continued winking.

"You seem to be grasping the rudiments," said Olivia, winking back smugly.

"Ah, you are flirting with me," Nebi said laughing.

"I am not," said Olivia again blushing. "I am teasing you," she said raising her eyes.

"Did you know your innocence is stirred within a pool of promiscuity that you are yet unaware of?" said Nebi, studying the young waitress, his eyes narrowed, holding his chin studiously as he went on, "Yet tends to ripple across the surface when you feel vulnerable, it makes you even more attractive." He slowly reached across and took Olivia's right hand, and kissed it. For a moment she stood speechless. "Now I am teasing you," he said bowing, they both laughed.

"I would like to see you again," said Nebi.

For a moment, Olivia paused, looking at him smiling. "I don't know what I am letting myself in for but I think I would like that too."

Nebi walked out into the cold night air, and for a moment he stood on the side of the pavement opposite the casino entrance and lit a cigarette. He ran his hand across the gun inside his breast pocket as if it offered some kind of reassurance towards his thoughts on what lay ahead.

"Good evening gentlemen," said Nebi as he walked up the steps. "Evening, sir," said the taller of the two tuxedoed men who opened the door. He walked into a bustling large ornate area, the space seemingly broken up by long marble-pillared columns. These slender, free-standing supports were jutted randomly around the large high-ceilinged room.

Blackjack and roulette tables were spread evenly around each side of the entrance area, several card tables lay scattered in numerical order around the middle, elegant women in cocktail dresses mingled with the more affluent customers, lingering intoxicated amidst the aphrodisiac of their money, surrendering to their wealth and vulgarity, inanimately masking their virtue.

Nebi walked across towards the bar area and ordered a brandy; a jazz pianist played nearby.

He sat for a while by a side table, overlooking the floor area, uniformed waitresses carrying silver trays, with short skirts, seemed to ooze amongst the crowds as if gliding on ice.

Nebi scanned the crowded tables; the atmosphere fizzled as if a match could be struck against it. He noticed several side rooms where high-stake card games were taking place. There were a couple of long-legged cocktail girls clutching bottles of champagne for the all-night parties that would go on behind those closed doors. James Hilary sat at a blackjack table; a very attractive tall raven-headed lady seemed to be nibbling his ear lobe while she rubbed his shoulders.

James Hilary had always liked the high life. It captured him, pulling him towards the more seedy side of its allure. Like a child locked within a fairground, whose attractions had long peeled and withered into an inevitable ugliness, yet he would remain to linger with an unnatural glee. He would relish the forbidden fruit of his moral contradictions as a government official. He had not been born into money, unlike many of his contemporaries. But what he lacked with the advantages of the right breeding he more than matched with brains. James Hilary had graduated from Cambridge University with a degree in history and politics. His left-wing political leanings had not gone unnoticed, and for a while he had borne an inner rage against his country, almost to the point of hatred at the snobbery within the system he worked, he knew his place and the hierarchy in his chain of command would not let him forget it.

Why should he be pigeon-holed beneath the public school pompous bastards who ran the country so ineptly, when he could name his price and receive what he deserved by giving up their identities to the other side. Why should he risk his life? only to remain a small link in this huge chain of nonentities, a "thank you, and well done", then a small pension to be content with. He had been introduced to an "underground" society, a deviant group of Marxist students, many of whom, along with him, had gone to work in the British government. One who was still active was head of the American department of the Foreign Office; another was First Secretary in Washington. All three were presently being investigated. James Hilary had embraced communism many years ago, and had been working as a Russian double agent before he had joined the British intelligence organisation; he had been responsible for countless deaths. He would do a "crossway" of information between three other agents, two British and one who was a Russian go-between.

Nebi sat and watched James Hilary for some time, he felt indifference for a man he had been ordered to kill. Killing him in a public place was meant to send a message to future would-be traitors, a message that the government could infiltrate any outside or inside conspiracies against the "system".

He carefully studied the exits, noticing the casino manager's office was situated at the end of a small corridor to the left of the bar area, that curved out of sight of the main entrance and exits.

A cashier's office stood opposite from where he was sat with what seemed like an iron door that was bolted from the inside, outside a man in a tuxedo that seemed ill fitting against his obvious bulk stood as imposing as he could. Nebi noticed what seemed to be fresh bruising around his knuckles.

He watched as a man and woman emerged from the manager's office, the man was carrying a bottle of champagne stopping every so often as the giggling woman snatched it from him and proceeded to gulp the contents, as she swayed unsteadily.

Nebi stood up, slipping his overcoat off and placed it across the back of his chair and walked back across the casino floor, he pulled a white napkin that was wrapped around an empty ice bucket on a nearby table placing it around his sleeve in the customary manner of a waiter, before retrieving the ice bucket and slowly strolling towards the bar. There was a line of ice buckets with fresh champagne with table numbers clipped to the side, he placed the empty bucket on a tray acknowledging one of two busy barmen, "Looks like we are in for a long one," said Nebi smiling as he nonchalantly picked up one of the ice buckets and walked away.

He walked across towards the corridor stopping outside the manager's office before tapping on the door a couple of times until it was obvious there was nobody inside. He turned the brass handle and pushed the door inwards as he walked into the room. There was a fading odour of perfume that lingered in the air.

A leather-bound swivel chair faced the window behind the large oak desk that stood in the middle of the office, and was occupied by a desk lamp and a phone. He pulled the phone off the hook, placing it on the desk. Nebi quickly walked around the office checking the bathroom before opening the door, glancing up and down the corridor, making sure it was clear, before slowly leaving closing the door behind him. He noticed the couple who had emerged from the office earlier were stood in a segregated area of the bar that was cordoned off, at the far side of the room.

Nebi pulled out a small silver hip flask from his inside pocket and walked towards the opening of a private gaming room, large purple drapes with gold tie-backs decorated the entrance in an exaggerated ornate grandeur. It was like an upmarket whorehouse.

Nebi slid his hand behind the curtains, emptying the contents of the flask down the back of the drapes before lighting a cigarette. He stood for a moment walking towards a crowded "craps" table, he watched as a fat American kept yelling with each throw of his dice to the cheers of the gathering crowd.

He walked back towards the opening and carefully flicked the lit cigarette behind the drapes at the bottom; it would take a few minutes to burn, he knew he had to be quick.

He walked towards the blackjack table where James Hilary was playing.

"Excuse me sir," said Nebi in a whispered tone leaning towards Hilary. "I have been instructed by the manager to inform you of an important phone call."

"Important?" said Hilary, slurping on the near-empty whisky glass, "Can't you see I'm winning? What's more important than that?" A large frown seemed to fall back against his receding hairline.

"I'm sorry, sir," said Nebi, "I have been instructed to inform you that it is Sir Reginald Frazier."

Hilary turned for a moment his eyes raised. "Really! Well it must be important if it's the old bastard himself." Hilary got up unsteadily, still clutching the whisky glass. "You will have to excuse me," he said bowing exaggeratedly as he pushed back his chair. "Get me a refill, my dear, oh and don't stick any of my chips where I will only find them later," Hilary said winking at his female companion.

"This way, sir," said Nebi. "You may take the call in private in the manager's office."

"I have not seen you before," said Hilary, placing an inquisitive hand on Nebi's shoulder.

"Why is that?" he asked frowning.

"I have not long started, sir."

"Where are you from?" asked Hilary.

"Egypt, sir. I have not been in England long."

"You do not appear to have been anywhere long, do you?" he said cynically.

Nebi could feel Hilary's wave of contempt weave around his foreign shoulders, yet contained a placable demeanour as he just smiled nodding in agreement.

The two men walked past the entrance to the gaming room, small plumes of smoke trickled up through the air but not enough to be noticed.

They slowly walked down the corridor towards the office, Hilary followed unsteady on his feet, at one point almost falling over.

"This way sir," said Nebi opening the door, fragments of the woman's perfume still hung in the air, from earlier.

Nebi glanced down the empty corridor before walking into the room and closing the door behind him.

James Hilary walked across towards the desk picking up the receiver. "Hello... hello! Sir Reginald, are you there?" For a moment, Hilary faced the window in silence as the buzzing tone at the other end of the line made it clear there was nobody there. He slowly lowered the phone.

"Who sent you?" he asked, turning around towards Nebi, who was attaching the silencer to the end of the pistol. "I said who sent y..."

Two shots thudded into Hilary's chest. He keeled forward, falling against the side of the desk, groaning, before rolling over onto the floor. Nebi quickly unscrewed the silencer putting the gun in his inside pocket, he glanced down at Hilary and did not enjoy watching the life leave this man as swift as a puff of smoke disperses into the air, as his sightless eyes seemed to stare back into the living world, staring back from the darkness up at him.

Nebi turned the handle slowly listening for any movement in the corridor but there was none. He quickly left the office rubbing the handle with the napkin when he heard a scream. He walked along the corridor; there was a surge of activity as he mingled through the gathering crowd across the casino floor. The purple drapes around the gaming room entrance were now completely ablaze. He noticed the two men, who were stood at the entrance earlier, were throwing buckets of water onto the fire, which had now began to creep across the walls, and around the door frame.

James Hilary had been a traitor, a "necessary kill", other people's lives had depended on the outcome, but as Nebi would discover, this would not always be the case.

FIVE

There would be many other "jobs" Nebi would do for the organisation down the years, not all involved killings. He would be asked to do clean ups, which involved the removal of bodies from various locations after a job was completed by a "co-worker" as they were known, co-workers in the same field never met.

For a while Nebi tried to detach himself from what he had become, he knew the world was a dangerous place, occupied by even more dangerous individuals. Olivia would become his release, his friend and companion, and the love of his life.

It had been on one of these jobs that his life had changed; he had been sent by the Foreign Office to Ravello situated along the Amalfi coast south of Naples in Italy. A hill town sheltered by the surrounding steep cliffs located on the small escarpment of Monte Latteri. A vast overlook dipped towards the coast south towards the Gulf of Salerno, overlooking the town of Amalfi below.

Nebi had spent three days tracking the individual that was "marked". His quest had come to an end in what looked like a derelict church situated north of the villa Cimbrone. The inward wind that would blow from between the surrounding cliffs ushered in from the gulf would whistle like faint screams, and frequently stirred the bell that hung above the old medieval church. The dull sound would rasp against the ancient walls in hollow tones as if in some way intent on beckoning the slow awakening of the dead, in the small graveyard across the north side of the town. Nebi watched as the man he was following forced the door of the church open and ran in. For a moment he stood as the sun sprayed down before him in an avalanche of heat; the still breeze windswept the dust across the back roads and along the streets which were eerily deserted.

Nebi walked towards the church, reaching for the gun inside his jacket. He pushed the thick wooden door noticing dust trickling from the edges as it creaked inwards. He stopped, lowering the gun by his side. He walked into the darkened interior where several windows had been boarded up; some planks had broken off and dangled, swaying in the ever-present breeze. Thin lines of sunlight poured across the stone floor, evoking swirling dust to flicker in the air. His eyes narrowed as he peered around the stillness, slowly walking along the centre aisle, again raising the gun, turning his head from side to side.

He noticed something move beside the altar; he shielded his eyes as the sunlight seemed more intense as he continued moving down the aisle. Nebi stopped as the brightness became too much to bear, he could almost feel the intensity of the heat on the back of his hand as he continued to cover his eyes.

He stopped turning his head to the side, the brightness seemed to be glowing across the walls, moving upwards towards the ceiling. He stopped, tumbling backwards against a bench, he could see the man standing at the edge of the aisle towards the centre of the altar just watching him, the light seemed to hover against him, moving across his shoulders, forming into something, that looked almost.... almost like wings.

Nebi felt a sudden coolness pour over him, and the hand he held above his eyes began to shake. His eyes blinked nervously as he frowned against the brightness, his hand sweated against the gun he was gripping tightly. He quickly moved towards the altar noticing the man was knelt beside it head bowed praying. Nebi again held the gun aloft, yet in the unnerving stillness he could feel his own beating heart thump in his ears. He did not feel at ease in this place, and for the first time he began to question himself, made him think of the kill, and it made him ask himself why?

Nebi stepped backwards lowering the gun by his side. The man continued to pray as if waiting for the inevitable. Nebi could not help noticing he was little more than a boy, a boy searching for sanctuary and hope within the house of God.

Again he could feel the contours of the gun handle, his forefinger caressing the rim of the trigger. One slight squeeze and he could walk away, back into the sunlight away from the unnerving stillness.

"You are free to go."

The man for a moment just stared ahead, before slowly turning his head towards Nebi.

"Did you not hear me? I said you can go."

Nebi watched as the man gripped the rail slowly rising to his feet. "Thank you," he said carefully backing away, tears had begun to roll down his face, yet they were not tears of fear. The man suddenly pointed towards Nebi, "I can see it all around you, the light of the Lord shines bright within you." There was a realisation and exhilaration in his eyes, "Like me you are a servant of God it is just that you are still unaware, and like me you yearn for answers."

Nebi watched as the man backed away from his would-be assassin, before running towards the door.

Unbeknown to Nebi the organisation always had a backup plan in case one of its employees had a "lapse" in concentration due to a sudden rush of conscience. The mark would not leave the island alive.

For a while Nebi stood within the silence of the small ancient church, his thoughts seemed interwoven in mass confusion inside his head. The interior had returned to its dark and gloomy overhanging. He looked upon the dust-covered crucifix that hung at the forefront of the altar, Christ outstretched in the ever-familiar pose. Cobwebs dangled outwards across the ceiling like thin strands of gold as sunlight sprayed across the white ageless face whose eyes were raised above, showing no torment, only pity, pity for those who had put him there. Nebi could still feel his beating heart thumping against his chest; he dropped the gun by his side, knelt down and began to pray.

SIX

Abigail Tripp had sat upon the edge of her bed for some time, gently rocking to and fro, her round hollow eyes staring blankly ahead. The self-made scars that were torn across her skin were still raw on her pale arms. Her long damp hair seemed to cling to her face as thin beads of sweat ran down her forehead.

The nightmares would come like subconscious trickles, then more frequent, building into raging storms, at first leaving her fragile body like a shipwreck as sleep became a trauma. The nightmares would become more bizarre, more real, as if the bizarre intertwined with reality when she awoke. Yet the fear had gone, the feeling of danger had gone, replaced by a feeling of control. She had felt something lurking amidst the chaos within her mind, something that had now begun to guide her.

Abigail was fifteen years old, and this had not been the first time she had tried to commit suicide, not the first time she had tried to escape.

She had been nine years old when the visions would come, when the terrible voices in her head would scream and rage in her confused darkened mind. As a child she witnessed the constant arguments between her parents, words that her father would scream like "possessed", "evil little bitch", "burned at birth" were common place. The arguments would get worse as her mother had tried to protect her, until after one of these arguments Abigail's father had beaten her mother so severely she had been left close to death. She had lain for almost two days with a fractured skull and several broken ribs unable to move. Abigail had tried to tend to her mother, tried to make the pain stop, but she had been hurt more than the child could know. Her mother had taken her final beating. She cradled her mother's head in her small arms, gently bathing the wounds, staring hard into her mother's sad eyes, waiting until they closed; Abigail knew they would not open again.

Abigail had sat with her dead mother until her father returned, she listened as he drunkenly fumbled with the lock before pushing the front door hard against the wall in the narrow hallway, she listened as he staggered upstairs, his footsteps thudding across the ceiling above as he went from room to room yelling and screaming her mother's name.

Abigail had waited at the bottom of the stairs until her father had slumped unconscious on his bed. She slowly climbed the stairs; clutching a heavy rusted can at her side, for a while she stood within the doorway, within the silence, just watching her father as he fell into a drunken slumber.

She slowly unscrewed the top of the can and placed it at the side of the bed, she walked across to her father's wardrobe, and the door creaked as she opened it. She carefully pulled out four of his ties. First she bound his ankles together, before threading one of the ties around the bedstead, completely binding his feet to the edge of the bed. Then she carefully tied his wrists, again threading the ties around the thick wooden poles of the headboard until both his arms dangled outwards. Abigail reached for the can and began pouring the contents across the edge of the bed and across her father's outstretched body, he murmured, moaning slightly, but still he did not wake. She had emptied three-quarters of the can across his body, the pungent odour of the highly flammable liquid hung across the darkened room, making her nostrils twitch slightly. The remaining liquid swirled inside the can, as she walked towards the top of the bed. Her father's head was turned to the side. She gently turned his head straight; he snored loudly, remaining in a deep sleep. Abigail reached for the can, holding the rim over her father's face before quickly tilting the contents into his mouth. She watched as he swallowed and gurgled, before making choking sounds, his body began to thrash against the bed twisting from side to side, his eyes flashed open. Abigail reached inside her pocket, opening the small box of matches. She stood back before striking one;

33

the glow flickered in the air, almost crackling, illuminating her father's face as he continued to cough, looking at her in horror.

She swayed the match across his face, taunting him, his terrified eyes seemed to scream out as they followed the flame, he continued to struggle gasping for air before she threw the match inside his mouth. For a moment she stood back, a strange elation seemed to pour through her, as she watched curiously, tilting her head slightly, as the muffled screams of her father were drowned out by huge flames that began to pour from inside his mouth, like giant illuminating spider's legs thrashing against the air as if about to burst from his head.

She walked back towards the doorway smiling as she watched her father die an agonising death. Abigail closed the door and walked down the stairs.

A neighbour found her next morning, sat rocking to and fro on the garden wall.

The two guards looked in through the peephole at the young girl.

"She's a weird one, gives me the fucking creeps," said the older of the two guards. He shook his head, "Something not right with her, I mean *really* not right," he continued, pushing the thin-rimmed glasses further up his nose. "She's been stuck in here indefinitely. This part of the hospital houses the real live ones," he went on. "Remember lad, they may walk around like zombies, high as kites on the concoction of shit these doctors give 'em, but just remember, first chance they get they will pull your fucking eyes out of your head before you can say lunatic."

"Yeah!" said James Portman, loosening his tie nervously, nodding his head as he looked at the dark desolate eyes of the young girl who just swayed to and fro.

The older guard scraped his keys across the door, smirking to himself; it was not the first time he purposely put the frighteners up a young wet-neck as he liked to call a new recruit, before walking down the corridor.

Portman continued to look through the small peephole. Abigail lifted her head smiling at him. Portman moved backwards uncomfortably. "Yeah a fucking weird one," he thought, covering the peephole and hurrying towards the other guard.

Abigail would lie in the darkness. At first the voices would ooze into her head, swirling like fading whispers in dreams, before building into screams and fierce rages. She had known the difference between good and evil. Good was something that left the world a long time ago, disappearing into the cosmos and beyond. Only evil existed within her world, and at first the evil poured from the voices in her head, beckoning her, taunting, until she welcomed the unnatural intrusion, until she became in complete control.

These entities that prowled across the oblivion of night would come; they would come from some other place. She relished these growling snarling creatures that hovered before her, the vile stench, as saliva dripped from their grotesque heads, these winged creatures forged against the darkness, their wings rasping against the walls. They seemed to hover in an eerie obedience before her, like huge lingering vultures stalking their prey.

She would have "glimpses" of her past. Flickers of remembrance of her so-called normal life, but she had long succumbed to the perpetual torment and bidding of her host.

Abigail rose from the bed and walked across towards the barred window, outside the still night wind blew; the trees rustled and shimmered, coated by the dull light of the moon as the clouds shifted across the sky.

She placed her fingers within the holes in the wire meshing that covered the inner window section, pulling tightly, until the tips of her fingers bled down upon the grey surface. Her eyes widening as she began to smile. Abigail fixed a glare upon the door, her face tightening; clenching her teeth, there was an uneasy silence before a strained click as the lock snapped. She held her hand up and the door slowly began to open outwards.

The figures still lingered, although they began to fade like shimmering apparitions that moved like puffs of smoke.

"Kill him, you must kill him."

Abigail moved towards the door, her dark vacant eyes stared ahead; she had to find the Christ.

Portman slowly tipped the coffee pot towards the cup.

"Hey! You're spilling it," said the elder guard as the coffee began to seep across his paper.

"I... I thought I heard something down there," Portman said, as he began dabbing the newspaper with his sleeve, turning his head peering down the corridor, placing the pot at the end of the table.

As the two men listened, an old Christmas song filled the air from a radio that had been placed upon a small stool at the side of the door to keep it open.

"Listen," said the elder guard, shaking his newspaper over the waste paper bin, the song petered out as he slowly turned the radio down. "I can hear it lad, the quieter it becomes the louder it gets."

"I don't understand," replied Portman, shaking his head.

The elder guard looked over at Portman wide-eyed, "The silence lad that eerie silence, just knowing the crazies are waiting to get at you can be deafening in here" he said tapping the side of his head with his forefinger.

"I am sure something moved at the bottom of the corridor."

"Clean up here, lad, and I will take a look." Portman watched the elder guard reach for his torch, as he began to walk down the dimly lit corridor.

"Fucking crazies," the elder guard thought, scraping the keys across their secure iron doors, another eighteen months and he would be free of this place, seemed like he'd been here a lifetime. Time has got a way of creeping up on you, not only the evident changes that come with age, but the changes occurring all around you, first it takes your loved ones, then it slowly beckons you, reeling you in towards the inevitable. If you're lucky you get to live a few years in retirement, a few years of freedom after a lifetime of looking after "fucking crazies", a lifetime of churning out a mundane existence of a nine-to-five regime, which can be like a living death.

There were times when he envied the "crazies", they existed within an inner world of their own making, maybe they were so detached from this life they lived within a place of green meadows and slow-flowing streams where there was no hurt, no pain, and once in a while they would awaken upon the cold morning of reality, back into this life, and the realisation of their existence, then literally piss and crap themselves, or worse, take a permanent way back by slitting their wrists.

His wife had died two years ago with what became a lingering death. Cancer had taken its grip before slowly ravaging her; all he could do was watch as she withered out of this life, hopefully to a better place.

He shone the torch across the corridor as he slowly tested each door; once in a while stopping and sliding open the peepholes. Some were just walking in circles around their room mumbling, a couple were sat at the bottom of their beds sobbing.

He dropped the torch, almost falling backwards, as he looked in on Henry Slater a prolific child sex killer, who was stood naked against the door masturbating.

"You filthy bastard!" yelled the guard, kicking against the door. He felt his mouth run dry as Henry Slater began to moan and writhe against the inside of the wall and doorway, groaning and panting like an animal, the guard felt sick. "If only I was carrying a gun I'd blow that sick bastard's brains out," he said as he stood in the middle of the corridor running his hand across his mouth and through his thinning grey hair.

He began to breathe heavily, "You should not let them get you like that, eighteen months of this shit, that's all, another eighteen months and they can all go and rot in hell along with this stinking hospital." The words trickled slowly from his mouth as he picked the torch up from the floor. His repulsion of Henry Slater burned in him, a huge knot turned in his stomach as he continued to walk down the corridor, and he noticed Portman rushing towards him. He waved the torch at him, "its okay, everything's okay, just another night at the zoo. And I am too old for this shit," he said to himself, shaking his head as he made his way towards the end. He tried the last few doors, which were all locked as they should be, except one; he frowned as he approached the doorway which was opened slightly. The elder guard shined the torch across the opening, he watched as the light slowly crept across the semi-darkened room as he pulled the door open. Abigail Tripp was stood holding a book, tearing out pages and stuffing them into her mouth; it was a copy of the Bible.

"What the hell is going on?" said the guard shining the torch across her face. The room looked like it had been ripped apart.

He checked the handle which just dangled loosely against the door, the steel shaft that ran through the outer iron reinforcement had somehow snapped off.

Abigail continued to tear the pages from the Bible placing them in her mouth, and spitting the contents across the room, she raised her head towards the guard. For a moment all he could do was look into her round hollow eyes which had become fixed on his.

Portman almost dropped the coffee pot as he attached it to its base placing the plug in the socket. The shrill scream that came from the bottom of the corridor forced an echo across the narrow walls as if rushing up towards him. Portman ran down the corridor, as he did there was several clicking sounds on either side as he quickly made his way towards the bottom.

"Is everything okay?" he shouted out, breathing heavy as he approached the open door. He could see his colleague's torch lying on the floor; he followed the light as it poured across the gloom, across his colleague's stricken body that lay limply against the inside wall. Portman moved slowly inside the room, it was if what he encountered seemed surreal, his eyes could see it clearly, yet his brain could not register what lay before him.

He looked upon his colleague's face; the dark hollow sockets where his eyes had been seemed to be looking back at him, a fine stream of blood oozed down each side of the dead guard's face like dark tears seeping into his shirt.

Portman staggered back towards the wall almost falling. Abigail Tripp appeared in the doorway. Portman noticed other figures walking down the corridor towards him. He scrambled to his feet running towards the fire door at the bottom end. He moved slowly, his legs seemed to weigh heavy against his body. As he tried to reach the door, they became rigid as if the blood that ran through them had turned to stone, and then he suddenly stopped.

His eyes raced across the walls and ceiling, he was unable to scream as the figures began to gather around him. Portman felt several hands moving over him, pulling and scratching against him, he tried to kick out but his legs would not move.

"Get away from me." He thrashed out with his arms frantically, a mixture of fear and adrenalin pumped desperately through his veins as he tried to scramble across the floor on his hands, dragging his body towards the sanctuary of the fire door and beyond. He reached for the large handle, pulling himself up, but he was quickly dragged back, they gathered around him trance-like, their faces expressionless against the hollow twilight, like some kind of lingering orbs… then they moved in.

Portman watched as more inmates poured into the corridor, they walked past Abigail Tripp who was stood in the foreground her head tilted as she smiled at him. A dark glimmer shone in her eyes as she watched the inmates as they began to bludgeon him, the smacks thudding against his body, continually, relentless breaking the bones in his legs and arms. At first the screams though went unheard, squealed like a train whistle in a tunnel. "Why did it take so long to die," he thought, as he looked at the world becoming blurred and abstract against the harsh reality that was destined to be his end; he lay helpless at the mercy of a bunch of frenzied "crazies". Finally the screams stopped, a naked Henry Slater wrenched the keys from Portman's corpse and walked across towards Abigail Tripp slowly handing them to her, his vile pathetic body standing trance-like in an unnatural obedience. She looked at him and he walked back towards the others.

Abigail Tripp walked silently towards the opposite side of the corridor. Before she reached the end, she turned to face her fellow inmates who were stood motionless like lost schoolchildren.

She raised her hand, her eyes narrowing as she concentrated against the ceiling and walls around them where they stood. A glow of light seemed to absorb them, curl around the walls, pulsating, becoming stronger, until it fizzled and crackled turning into groups of flames, licking against the air as is began to rush across the walls and ceiling, building into a raging fire. There was no screams as they remained still, the flames devouring their bodies, burning them where they stood like wilting candles. Still no one screamed. Maybe they had already gone to that other place of green meadows and slow-flowing streams. There would be no survivors.

SEVEN

The siren continually screeched across the night air, in an annoying reverberant howl as the ambulance pulled to a halt. Two of the street lights did not work, giving an overview of gloom that fell along the side alleyway that was situated towards the rear of several derelict buildings. These buildings lay desolate, devoid of life or substance, eerily hanging like abandoned carcases against the backdrop of the surrounding city.

A young police officer had begun cordoning off the area with yellow tape; a crowd of people had already started to gather upon the periphery of the crime scene, as the fervent activity, and mounting tension in the atmosphere stirred their curiosity. They were kept a safe distance as more police officers emerged upon the area. Two CSIs were carefully taking photographs of everything in and around the victim, while another forensic scientist was carefully examining the body. Everyone who entered needed special clearance as the concept was, every time somebody enters an environment, something is added to it, and also inadvertently removed.

Killings were not uncommon in this part of town, a drug addict or prostitutes were regarded as run-of-the-mill human garbage, whose trades could lead them to this eventuality. Yet the victim was neither of these, although the manner and ferocity in which he died was perplexing to say the least, as his head had almost been completely torn off, as he had been somehow pinned, spread-eagled upside down to the wrought-iron gate of the nearby church, and he had what was left of a priest's collar on.

Jack Bannerman's hand shook slightly as he clenched his fist and began punching down on the steering wheel. He observed himself in the driver's mirror, running his left hand across his unshaven face and through his hair. His reflection had a look of disgust, amidst the sadness his eyes held, they still bore the anger he felt, yet it was a look that did not care as he studied his face, he had stopped caring a long time ago.

The world had turned slowly for Jack Bannerman in the last few years. He had made detective inspector by the time he was thirty-five.

Lady luck had walked alongside him, guiding him, until she would bare her cold shoulder and sharp teeth, tearing into his world. Marriage had given him a beautiful wife, and eventually a beautiful daughter who became his life. He worshipped the little girl they called Ashley. It was not until she was four that she became ill with leukaemia, a disease that suppresses the production of normal blood cells, and in Ashley's case it held a bleak prognosis, as nine times out of ten it proves a killer.

Jack was hopeful, the little girl was a fighter, tough like him, he was sure she would pull through. For the first time in his life, Jack Bannerman had begun to pray, he would sit in his local church for hours, kneeling, begging, "Please Lord, I know we have not talked much before, and I had little cause to call on you, but please, I need you now, don't take my little girl." Bannerman would weep in the still silence of the church.

Eventually he would sleep in the hospital chapel refusing to go home, feeling that God would cast some miracle and his daughter would get better, but she did not.

"Don't worry Daddy, I am not frightened," said the little girl, holding her father's hand, her eyes sparkled amidst the pallor of her grey complexion. "God has told me, I don't need to be afraid, and he said so in my dreams. I will live on in your dreams, Daddy." Ashley died two hours later.

And in some way his wife had also been a victim in this tragedy, retreating deep within her-self, refusing to accept what had happened, blaming him, cursing him.

He turned the wipers on to clear the windscreen, and the flashing siren forced him to shield his eyes. His head throbbed slightly; Bannerman needed his usual fix. He reached into his inside pocket, pulling out a small silver container.

Quickly undoing the top he began gulping down the contents, barely flinching as he had long become accustomed to its harsh taste as the liquid oozed down his throat, burning as it fell down into the pit of his stomach. He knew that drink was something that cocooned him from the reality he struggled to face, and he knew in some way it was a coward's substitute for the weaker minded, and this was something he was not.

He turned the key and the engine fell silent and for a moment he sat in the silence of the car amidst all the chaos occurring outside. Bannerman took a deep breath as he opened the car door, "You okay Jack?" asked his sergeant who was walking across towards him.

"Do I look okay?" he replied climbing out of the car seat.

"Maybe you came back too soon Jack," said Foster. "These things take time."

Bannerman looked at his sergeant sharply. "Look Jack, I don't mean to overstep the mark, we have been friends a long time, but you don't look in great shape, when was the last time you slept?" Foster continued, handing Bannerman his carton of coffee. "Drink it, Jack, you smell like a brewery and look like shit."

Bannerman sipped the coffee refraining from answering back as he knew Sergeant Foster was right.

"What have we got here?" he asked, as he looked across at the gathering police officers. He noticed a young female constable emerging from a side entrance; she was clearly shaken and appeared to have been physically sick, as she pressed a handkerchief to her mouth, slightly flushed, and making her way back towards her colleagues.

"You better come this way Jack, It looks like it could be a priest," said Foster, as he led Bannerman towards the corpse. "Looks... like a priest," he replied raising the crime tape as they walked through. Bannerman frowned as he studied what lay before him.

"Yeah," said Foster. "Look!" He pointed at the dead man, as the head was leaning awkwardly towards one side, with what was left of a priest collar on; it had almost been severed from the shoulders.

"Where was God when you needed him pal?" Bannerman said, as he crouched beside the corpse.

"Good to see you back working Jack," said Kate Ross, who was examining the body. Bannerman felt uncomfortable at the sympathy he detected in her eyes.

"Well no prizes for guessing what killed him," said Foster shrugging his shoulders. "The severity of the wound to the throat is the obvious cause," said Ross. "The thyroid gland and the right common carotid artery were completely severed, almost torn out." She shook her head sighing, "The barbarity of murder never ceases to amaze me."

"This could be almost described as overkill," she continued, rising to her feet, "almost animalistic."

"What's this?" asked Bannerman pointing towards the centre of the dead man's chest. There was a fine puncture wound approximately eight inches above the abdomen.

"We won't know until we get him back to the lab," said Kate Ross. Bannerman noticed the man's left hand was clenched shut; he knelt down and began to discreetly prise the fingers open. Noticing a folded up piece of paper that appeared to have traces of blood across it, Bannerman pulled it from the man's hand and slipped it in his pocket.

"My guess is he was killed somewhere else," he said pulling a crumpled cigarette packet from inside his coat. "Yes I agree," said Ross pulling off the surgical gloves. "The church is being searched extensively as we speak."

"Am I missing something here?" asked Foster with a puzzled look of incredulity across his face.

"The blood from the initial wound across the torso has dried, giving a time-lapse," said Kate Ross. "Also," she continued gesturing with her pen, "when the wound to the throat occurred, and the jugular vein punctured, the blood would have sprayed outwards across the road surface, and there would have been traces across these walls, yet there was no other trace other than what you see on the body, and ground; he was killed somewhere else."

"Yeah and put here, somehow," Bannerman said curiously studying the angle of the body that was pinned upside down to the gate.

Bannerman lit his cigarette as he watched the zip of the body bag pulled open.

"Don't worry, Daddy, I am not afraid, God has told me in my dreams."

His daughter's words would never leave him. Kate Ross gave the signal for the body to be removed. "Why the hell a priest?" said Foster shaking his head.

"That's simple enough," replied Bannerman, "because the Lord, your God, allows it."

"How's Ally?" asked Kate Ross gently squeezing his arm. For a moment Bannerman avoided her eyes as he equally tried to avoid the question, instead staring along the ground before pulling away uneasily as he slowly ran the toe of his shoe along a patch of dry blood that twinkled, sparkling against the dark amidst the earlier rainwater that had fallen in the afternoon.

"She's still the same," he replied. "Locked in her own world, blames me, I guess, blaming me is in some way her release, her way of living through the pain."

"You can't blame yourself Jack, what you did was for the best, she needed help to cope with this tragedy, and she needed to be *admitted!* If only for her own sake, and yours." Bannerman closed his eyes as *that* word seemed to wrench at him, did he really have to be reminded that he had his wife admitted to a secure hospital, as if she had not been through enough.

"How do you live through the pain Jack?" Ross asked looking into his eyes, deep, beyond the sadness.

"I don't," he said sharply, "I exist through it, from day to day." He lit another cigarette.

"Well if you need anything Jack, you know where I am," said Kate sincerely, as she began to walk across to her car.

"Hey Jack, are you going back to the station?" asked Foster blowing into his cupped hands.

"Yeah maybe later, something I need to check out first."

45

"That checking does not involve a bar I hope eh... Jack."
Bannerman watched his sergeant nod his head, raising his eyes
knowingly, before patting his shoulder and walking off towards
his car.

A few police officers remained as they continued to search
the alleyways, their torches cutting through the gloom at the
other end. He looked around before reaching to his pocket for
the folded up piece of paper and held it before him. Slowly he
opened it; the writing looked to have been written in blood, the
priest's blood. He squinted at the lettering, ANNO DOMINI.
He again looked around puzzled, placing the piece of paper
in a plastic evidence bag, normally he would have done some
much-welcomed overtime in a bar as Foster had suggested, but
something stirred within him about the events of this night that
bothered him, his detective hunches were on overdrive, if he had
nothing else in his life, there was still "the job". He pulled the
collars of his coat around his neck, as he walked towards his car
he shuddered for a moment, he wanted to think it was the icy
blasts of winter in the air but he was not so sure.

EIGHT

CHRISTMAS NIGHT

"Eloi, Eloi Lema Sabachthani!" The words had been yelled out continually in the last couple of minutes in random outbursts, like a drum roll of vitriolic obscenities, which filled the small room.

"He's been in and out of consciousness all day," said Ethan Cole, who'd been put in charge of Gabriel Salmach. "We have had a doctor to him; he falls asleep then starts ranting these same words over and over." Ethan shook his head, wiping his brow that twinkled with perspiration. "Man…" he continued, "I did not know what to do, that's why I called you."

Ethan had only worked at the hospital for nine months, having moved over to England from Philadelphia in the United States of America. He was a likeable large African American with an infectious laugh, his nature was filled with both consideration and care, which became endearing to all who encountered him, and he could be considered as one of life's good guys. He could be classed as overweight, due to his one and only vice – food. Yet he liked to describe himself as "well stacked", "big is healthy," he would say, "even if it is in all the wrong places."

Ethan wiped down Gabriel's brow.

"I never seen him like this before," he continued frowning at the priest.

Father Jonathan Creegan had stood in silence as he watched Ethan try to stir Gabriel from what seemed like a restless haunted sleep.

They watched as Gabriel's head turned uneasily against the headrest of the electric wheelchair, but still he did not awaken.

47

"Hey Gabe! Come on man, you in there?" Ethan said gently tapping the side of Gabriel's face.

Ethan had spent the early part of his life looking after his mother, after she was shot in a botched liquor store hold up. Two teenage thieves held up the store, one of them, wielding an automatic handgun, threatened the storekeeper, while his accomplice jumped over the counter and proceeded to empty the cash register. It had been the third time in as many months the store had been robbed, and this time the storekeeper was ready. He was ready to nail the bastards. The shotgun was carefully concealed under the bottom shelf of a cigarette rack attached by two hooks only a couple of feet away. The storekeeper's fingers began to tingle; it was as if he would will the gun into his hands.

The elderly black woman who had only gone into the store as an afterthought to buy her son a treat of his favourite candy bars had begun to whimper in fear.

"Shut up bitch," said the youth who still had the gun pointed at the storekeeper. The next few seconds seemed to blur into a puff of slow motion, the robber who was emptying the cash register was blown across the counter, and his friend began to fire at random, hitting the storekeeper in the arm before being shot dead himself. The elderly black woman lay awkwardly at the top of an aisle, she was alive but bleeding heavily from the base of her back, a stray bullet had caused a major lesion to the spinal cord, completely severing it. Although she would live, she would suffer complete paralysis to the lower body.

Ethan, who was an only child, and had never known his father, now had to become the man of the house, it was something he embraced without any hesitation, or without any question as the devotion he held for his mother surpassed any obstacle.

Ethan was a bright child, and a good student, he was always eager to learn, he wanted to learn about his mother's paralysis to understand her disability. He wanted to know how best he could help, he devoured books on the subject, yet his being there was all the help his mother needed, right up to the day she died.

He earned a place to Sergeant College at Boston University for occupational therapists and rehabilitation counselling. Supporting himself with various jobs from barman, dog walker, street cleaner to hotel janitor, whatever he did it was with a hundred per cent application, as if it was the most important job in the world, and whatever obstacle life put before him, he faced with a smile, however poor and penniless at times he was, he somehow felt the richest man on the planet.

He would relish all things around him. Ethan could only see the good in everything; this was not out of naivety, but there seemed to be purity in his soul, in his being, that looked beyond the bad of the world. His appreciation of life outweighed the everyday things we take for granted, where our eyes look upon but do not see, and our hands touch but do not feel, yet he was very aware of the great sadness in life that surrounds us every day, and he wanted to help, help ease the sadness in others.

He had gained a master of science in occupational therapy, Ethan's decision to leave the hospital where he had worked for the past two years seemed precipitant but he knew he had to go, he knew he must go. The post at St Michael's in England, another part of the world, would not only prove a challenge, but in some way a conscientious endeavour or effort at controlling the unturned chapters of his life.

"You any idea what those words mean, Father?" asked Ethan, as he continued to dab Gabriel's brow turning to face the priest.

Father Creegan bit down on his bottom lip, as he shook his head.

"When did he first say this?" he asked, frowning and placing his hat at the side of the bed.

"I... I have never heard it before today, Father," said Ethan sensing something disturbed the priest.

Father Jonathan Creegan sat at the edge of the bed, crossing his hands over his lap, for a moment he just stared in silence. *"My God, my God, why have you forsaken me?* This is what it means," said the priest. "It is mentioned in the Bible, the Gospel according to Mark." The two men for a moment just looked at each other in silence, a different kind of confusion simultaneously stirring in their minds. Gabriel began to stir and murmur, before slowly opening his eyes.

Graham Manning

Gabriel Salmach blinked as he moved his right hand slowly towards his face; his hand began to shake as his forefinger rubbed across his eye ducts from the bridge of his nose, causing a redness to form just above his cheeks.

Gabriel was a paraplegic; he suffered from complete paralysis of the lower body. His injury, a result of the car crash that killed his parents, completely severed his spine just below the thoracic region, towards the base of his back. The spinal cord, which is part of the central nervous system, and independently controls numerous reflexes, and complete paralysis, meant he could feel no sensation or voluntary movement, resulting in the trauma suffered below the spinal lesion. Gabriel had long given up ever trying to walk again, and for a long time he had wished he had died along with his parents.

After the initial trauma and shock, then came the fear, the fear of entering the outside world as somebody that was "incomplete", as a young boy he had become bitter and resentful, at first not responding to the treatment and help that was meant to aid the psychological damage an injury like this can cause.

For a time Gabriel had gone deep within himself, questioning the "cards he had been dealt". Some resign themselves to the fact of life's unlucky hand, and can fall deeper and deeper in, and there are some patients who look for other ways out, some like Gabriel's friend Emily White.

Emily had been a promising showjumper, and was tipped to make the England team. At the 1984 summer Olympics at Los Angeles her horse, Firebrand had spooked during a three-day event trial, throwing her in mid-jump. Emily had landed on a fence, badly breaking her back. After several months in hospital, she had been given the devastating news that she would never be able to walk again.

Emily had been brought into the occupational therapy and rehabilitation centre at St Michael's, she was an attractive seventeen year old whose life seemed destined for greatness, until fate intervened, it was as if two worlds collided within her life, and she was left in a dark place, while the other moved on. Even

50

though many patients would adjust both physically and psychologically, going on to lead full and rewarding lives, Emily's rehabilitation would prove slow and painful, it would also prove futile, as she retreated within herself. To rehabilitate decisions have to be made by the individual. Her father had pushed for advanced treatment and money was of no object. Clinical trials into new treatments were still some way into the future. Slowly there would be an improvement. On the last day of Emily's life she seemed at her happiest that she had been for months, her parents and friends had visited during the afternoon and was amazed that she had been in great spirits.

"You look great love," said her mother, wheeling her towards the edge of the spacious grounds towards a large oak tree that spiralled outwards offering a welcome shade from the warm sun as flickers of light poured through its branches that hung, twisting like cracks across the pale blue sky.

"I will be okay, Mother," said Emily. "You and Dad don't need to worry, really I will be fine."

Her mother kissed her on the forehead; there was a slight quiver of her lips as she looked down at her daughter.

"I know love. You know we love you, don't you?"

"Of course I do," replied Emily, gripping her mother's hand, slowly rubbing it across her cheek, "and I love you both, never forget that."

Emily had been found next morning with her wrists slit, she had bled to death during the night.

"Hey man," said Ethan, "good to have you back, you have been out for hours." Gabriel shuffled uneasily for a moment, before slowly turning the lever that controlled the wheel-chair, he glanced towards the priest who was scrutinising him.

"Hello, Father, it is good to see you."

"Thank you, it's good to see you, Gabriel."

"Ethan, may we have some coffee?" asked the priest.

"Sure," said Ethan. Pouring some water from a container and placing it upon a side table besides Gabriel. "Tell you what," he continued, "bet I could rustle a couple of beers up, my authority is like my weight round here, getting bigger." Ethan laughed out loud, as he acknowledgcd the subtle request for privacy nodding across at the priest, as he left the room.

"Father, I am scared," said Gabriel, beads of sweat began to flicker upon his brow. "Something… something's happening to me and I cannot explain it."

Father Creegan pulled a chair that was placed by the side of the window and sat beside Gabriel. For a moment, the priest studied him; Jonathan Creegan had known the hard side of life. Born in Dublin, he had grown up witnessing the many atrocities that humans can inflict on each other. Two of his brothers had been hard-line republicans, "Soldiers of the cause", before being ambushed by a British covert unit that had been placed in Northern Ireland as a "sleeper squad". His brothers had been killed before they could execute a car bombing campaign around the provinces outside the capital, aimed at military personnel. He had decided early on to follow a different route, to do something against the devastation that surrounded him, destroying family after family, dcath could not be the only solution.

His calling had always been there, in a way the compulsion ran deep within him like a thirst, which was partially quenched when he joined the priesthood. His search for answers lay beyond the hatred in these men's hearts, beyond the hell that can sometimes transpire upon the earth. The quest was his life's search for the good in man he felt that God had given us. Father Creegan had tried through the spiritual approach to infiltrate their reasoning, tilting the course of their free will; he sought to reach into this "core" of evil that was bound by this "cause" and perpetrated with naïve diligence. Yet evil would always prevail, its darkness would smother what shadows of reason that would fall in the light.

"Gabriel I feel the Lord moves through us, works through us and everyday he speaks through our actions, through the way we live. He is the very essence of life itself."

"He is all things," continued the priest, "and we are him in his own image, for the greater good or greater evil."

"Father," smiled Gabriel, "I am only too aware of this, more than you could know, that's my problem."

"What do you mean?" asked the priest frowning.

"I… I feel things Father, all things, I can see clearly like never before in my life."

"After the resentment you felt because of your injuries, the hatred in your heart could be finally melting away," said the priest, raising his eyes at Gabriel. "Please excuse the cliché, he went on, but you have found God, hey! It can happen to the best of us." Again the priest raised his eyes smiling.

"No, you do not understand, Father, it is not resentment, I feel and see everything, when I lie awake at night, I can hear the grass breathe, the soft voices in my head, are the thoughts of those around me, I can hear the birds sleeping in the trees, I can hear the dawn light approach, soft like whispers pouring across the darkness, I can hear the sprays of the sun warming the ground, rising across the stems of flowers. I feel the anger of the wind, as it roars across the still night, relinquishing into silence as it fades away, it is not hatred that guides my heart."

Father Creegan ran his right hand through his hair, as he rose to his feet.

"I do not feel fearful of the future any more, like I once did," said Gabriel. "I cannot explain it but something has changed in me, and it continues to do so as we speak."

Gabriel turned the wheelchair towards the priest. On the many visits the priest had made to Gabriel Salmach, as he did to many of the patients at St Michael's, the one thing he always noticed, especially in new patients, was the yearning within their eyes, and it always said the same thing to him, why me? This inward desperation, or shock to the system, would eventually ease, as the patient comes to terms with the disability and learns to live with it. Yet as the priest studied Gabriel, he could not help feel a strange sense of foreboding trickle over him, he gripped his hands together as he tried to hide the shiver that ran through him.

"I am going to have a different doctor look in on you, Gabriel," said Father Creegan. "I'm getting concerned."

"There is no need, Father," he replied, smiling at the priest's concern mixed with his confusion.

"But... but you don't sound well, Gabriel,"

"You say I have found God, I have been reborn..."

Gabriel turned the wheelchair towards the window; the purple veil of night seemed to pour across the glass, as the surrounding trees clung like a million veins against the fading blue sky. "Tonight you will have a visitor Father. And he needs your help and concern more than I do."

The priest frowned. "What... what do you mean? Who shall visit me Gabriel?"

"Someone who is a little bit lost, someone who is searching his understanding of God's will, he needs you Father." He turned to face the priest, "And you will need him."

Ethan opened the door with his free hand, carrying the tray of coffee in the other.

"Hey you guys, look what I found lingering in one of the cupboards, just crying out to be eaten, and I am ready to ohhblige," he said wide-eyed, smiling.

He placed the tray upon the table; there was a plate with a large half-moon of chocolate cake layered in almond speckles.

"People should know better than to leave things like this around when old Ethan's in town," Ethan laughed to himself, as he began to slice the cake before acknowledging the uneasy silence in the room. "Hey fellas, I might be mistaken, but today is Christmas right?"

"No you are not mistaken, Ethan," said Gabriel, pushing the lever and slowly the motorised wheelchair whirred towards the tray of coffee. "The world is continually wedged between good and evil, Father, as was the Son of God when he was crucified between Dismas and Gestes, the two thieves who were to die alongside him," Gabriel continued. "As the story goes, Dismas the penitent thief in death had found his faith and asked the son, to remember him in his kingdom, thus welcoming death as a mere transition towards eternal life, whereas Gestes swam within a sea of antipathy and doubt."

Father Creegan sipped his coffee as he studied Gabriel. "The unfortunate scenario," said the priest, "human antipathy towards the good of the world, and what is right has only prevailed, is deep-rooted in all of us and continues to grow, as many continue to swim within that sea." The priest paused for a moment before continuing, "It seems evil sits heaviest on the scales of our free will."

"Hey man, this is deep," said Ethan, "but surely the get-out clause is that we have been given choice, the freedom of choice?"

"Yes," replied the priest, "and maybe that is the burden, as we continually, through our 'choice', kill and wage war upon each other, our will sets us apart from the animals of the earth, our freedom of decision and choice, yet at times our morals seep lower than the rats that crawl through the sewers below us."

"But your belief is beyond that," said Gabriel, "and your faith is strong."

The priest gave a wry smile, "Erm... I'm not so sure," he replied, "even a priest's faith is hard to sustain, given the atrocities we are forced to witness day after day across the world. I sometimes, even after all these years, question God's way."

"Surely that's what makes you human?" said Ethan. "I mean, are we really equipped to understand how the big guy upstairs works?" he continued raising his eyes as he bit into the cake, part of it crumbling falling into the coffee cup.

"There was never a night when I did not lie awake and question the way of God," said Gabriel, "and if you pardon another cliché," he said smiling, "question him to why his 'mysterious ways' had left me like this? Crippled before my life had really started. Yet," he continued, "I feel that is of no importance, it has become irrelevant to my being, the lesson learned is I exist, I am alive. The life God has given me flows as free as a river or lake. And yes, he went on, I do, in a way feel reborn, reborn to the understanding and realisation of God the Father, his reasoning of fate, and the reasoning of our existence."

"Well!" said the priest. "Your understanding and eloquent... portrayal of this inner reasoning, you seem to have found is very impressive, Gabriel," he nodded reaching for his hat.

"I will visit you tomorrow," said the priest, as he walked towards the edge of the bed. Father Jonathan Creegan felt concerned, the foreboding he felt earlier still swirled within him like dark flowing water without a source or an end.

"Ethan, would you walk me to the door?" he asked as he began putting his coat on.

"Sure, Father," said Ethan, brushing a pile of crumbs under the bed with his foot. "Keeps the cleaners busy, eh!" Ethan winked at the priest.

"I will speak with you soon, Father," said Gabriel, as he turned the wheelchair towards the window, the inky black darkness seemed to throb against the glass, there was a slight glimpse of the moon as the clouds shifted, and it looked like a rip in the sky.

"I'm worried," said the priest, as they walked along the corridor. "He does not seem himself."

"Hey Father, that's the most I have ever heard him say since I worked here."

"Yes, that's what is bothering me, it's what he said. You have my number, Ethan, you must ring me if there are any more of these episodes, whatever the time, you must ring me, do you understand?"

"Sure thing, Father," replied Ethan. "Hey, you don't think he's gonna do something stupid?" Jonathan Creegan placed his hand upon Ethan's shoulder. "No I don't think it's as simple as that," replied the priest, turning walking through the swing door.

NINE

There is something about death apart from the inevitable, the finality of one's transition from this life, which is almost enchanting. And depending on whom, what, or how, it can sometimes feel almost inviting. Like the very first time we could feel the warmth of our mother's embrace as we were thrust into this world, and such an embrace we so yearn for as we are about to depart it. Or maybe we are to become a moveable feast, rendered, hurtling like some astral transient body jettisoned out of this living mortality towards the great jaws of an infinite beyond. Like a sacrificial Passover from life to death, our existences to shimmer away like a puff of smoke. Our memories all but relinquished to fading conversations kept alive by conjecture or speculative rhetoric that will mould our being in this life, for the good or the bad, towards the final departure, leaving all but our remains. Our remains too lie deep beneath, embroidered by dead leaves upon a cold ground where unsubstantial feet may tread.

Or is this afterlife in some way the great waiting room between past, present and future lives? Our actions shall dictate which doorway we shall wait by, and eventually walk through. And our actions shall dictate, but without our choice, our passing. Our memories are for this one time, this one life we are now leaving, not the thousands of existences our spirit could have endured and may endure again and again. The beckoning of our spirit is the repayment of our lives, and our legacies. Are we to sleep a thousand great sleeps? Before which we are called upon to walk through this glimpse of a living existence once again, within a different time, or place.

Or is the dust from our bones relinquished into the nothingness we came?

Sergeant Foster walked down the long corridor towards the mortuary, and for a few moments he just stood outside the door. He ran his hand across his mouth which was dry, then clasped them together tightly as if in prayer. Fine beads of sweat glistened upon his forehead and across his top lip. He looked along the vacant corridor before walking across to a water dispenser, pulling a plastic cup from the bottom of the chute and flicked the switch, the water gushed against the inside of the cup swirling around the small container, quickly filling, some rolled across his hand as it poured over the top of the cup. The cool water felt good as he ran his wet hand across his forehead wiping his face which had begun to flush slightly. He drank the water before crushing the plastic cup and throwing it in the bin.

He walked back facing the door, which was marked CONFERENCE ROOM – PRIVATE. Rooms like this are often kept hidden for obvious reasons; he recalled one of the examiners telling him on a previous visit, of a workman stumbling in while an autopsy was taking place, he used the slice and dice American term because he preferred it, and the sight of the Y shaped incision across the corpse's chest and the exposure of several vital organs caused the man to hyperventilate almost dying. Foster shook his head at the thought.

The autopsy room, where the examiner did his work, stood between the mortuary and a store room. He walked across to the mortuary door pushing it open, a strong odour of clinical sterilisation poured out across the hallway; it was a smell he hated. Foster took several deep breaths before entering. On the facing wall were the "coolers" where the bodies were stored.

Sergeant Foster had witnessed death many times, in his job it was an occupational hazard, and he had recently found a man battered to death in an alleyway, his head had been left like the aftermath of a collision with a juggernaut, and it had taken a while for the sound of the flies buzzing to leave his ears. He began to breathe heavily as his mind opened the cooler doors and slowly the trays began to slide out before him, the decaying bodies open-eyed, grinning, observing him, and relishing his fear. He backed away almost stumbling.

"Is this it?" Foster said to himself. "We have to go through all the shit this crap hole of a world can throw at us then we end up here." Again he ran the back of his hand across his forehead, "Why the shit do I come here?" he asked himself again shaking his head.

In the middle of the room was a gleaming stainless steel table with a drain in the centre, although the whole area had been cleaned and sterilised many times, when he looked at the drain and saw hair and unidentifiable sludge, and an orange brown stain was caked around the drainage tube, and what looked like ground bone, the saliva in his mouth began to taste bitter evoking a slight swirling in his stomach, he quickly held his mouth.

"Breathe heavily… breathe heavily," the thoughts flashed in his head like flickering neon signs. Foster gripped the edge of a chest level tray where organs would be placed, and began to breathe in steady bursts.

"Ah Sergeant Foster," said Doctor Kate Ross as she walked into the room; she had pretended not to notice Foster's uneasiness as she proceeded to pull off the surgical gloves, the fingers on each glove was a dull slimy red. "I take it you have come about the priest?" she said smirking as Foster began wiping his brow.

"Well! I have not come to break a picnic hamper out now have I?" the sergeant replied shaking his head. "Where is he?"

Doctor Ross walked over to a shelf that stored several autopsy implements, she picked up a large thick needle, and a hand-held bone saw.

"He is in the other room," she replied, "we have just finished an external examination of the body," she went on running her thumb along the large thick needle. "There seems to be no next of kin, as we have only received lawful consent, there is always a time issue with these things," continued the doctor walking towards the door.

"Yeah I know," said Foster frowning at the stainless steel table. "The usual red tape bullshit, has he been identified?" he asked walking across towards the coolers.

"We have been busy these last couple of nights," Ross went on pointing towards the cooler doors. "The occupants in those are what is left of some of the patients of that psychiatric hospital that went up in flames, burned to a crisp is an understatement, would you like to take a look?" She pulled off her glasses and held them before her examining the lenses, before wiping them with the end of her sleeve. "More like a human barbeque," she went on, ignoring the distain that befell Foster's face as he edged uneasily away from the cooler doors.

They walked across towards the autopsy room, the prevailing mood on entering this area is one of curiosity, it seeps scientific interest, this is what Sergeant Foster found hard to fathom, what kind of moron delved around in a person's blood and guts to quench a scientific thirst and call it a job?

Foster could almost taste the fillings in his teeth as a pathologist had just finished cutting through the skull of another corpse with a vibrating saw. The pathologist smiled as they entered the room.

"Like I said, we have only done an external examination of the body," said Doctor Ross. One of the technicians was taking photographs of the priest as they walked towards the centre of the room, while another body was being wheeled away. Foster frowned as he witnessed the wound across the dead man's throat.

"Do we have a time of death?" asked Foster, reaching into his pocket for a handkerchief as he began to cover his mouth. "All we can be is approximate, about fourteen hours before he was found," replied Doctor Ross. "Yet we can say that whoever or whatever did this possessed great strength," said the pathologist, pointing towards the wound with a scalpel. "You see," she continued, "the contents of the throat were completely torn out."

"I can see that," interrupted the sergeant. "Your average maniac, his mind on overdrive with drugs, is capable of anything."

"Maniac I agree," replied the pathologist frowning. "Yet this one possessed what I can only describe as claws or talons, as there are uniformed slashes across the throat causing deep incisions that had to be something other than a human hand or singular instrument."

60

"Maybe we have a wolf man running around," said Foster, raising his eyes.

"What we do have is a human being who met a horrific death," replied Doctor Ross. "We must not forget that." Foster paused for a moment, before nodding apologetically. "What about that?" he asked pointing to the incision above the abdomen.

"It appears to be a single knife wound by a narrow serrated edged blade, longer than your average flick knife, but too short to be a sword."

"So it seems we have some 'nut job' that cannot decide whether to pull a guy's throat out or stab them first," Foster said.

"That's your job," said Doctor Ross smiling.

"This world never ceases to amaze me," Foster continued as he scrutinised the body. "We live in a cesspit of wall-to-wall nutcases, it becomes hard to tell which of us is looking in or out of the cage, and even priests are not safe."

"You have a cynical view of the human race sergeant," said Ross looking over the rim of her glasses at him.

"Not cynical doctor," said Foster, "in this job it becomes hard to see beyond the bad in people when you are continually met with the atrocities we so-called humans are capable of, then!" He continued shaking his head, "Then this!" he said raising his arms, "this... this finality of life." He paused, a look of disgust on his face, "The thought that one day some bastard could put me there," he went on pointing towards the body, "lying pathetic on some slab, served up like a course of stale meat on a platter." For a moment he paused wiping his brow. "I... I'm sorry," said Foster, "I didn't mean to..."

"It's okay," said Ross, in a reassured tone, "the sight of death effects people in different ways. His only consolation is he is in a better place."

"It just kind of puts things into a bleak perspective, of what to look forward to, I suppose that's my fear, what if it ends here." Foster turned walking towards the door.

Kate Ross followed the sergeant towards the exit.

61

"I am concerned about Jack," she said, opening the door. They walked into the passageway; the sound of a bone saw whirred against the walls like the propellers of a small plane.

"Yeah me too," replied Foster turning towards the doctor. "I think he should have taken more time out after what happened, he is hanging out with his namesake, who is also very bad company when they get together." Doctor Ross frowned puzzled. "A certain Mr Daniels goes by the first name of Jack." Foster's eyes rose as he nodded at the doctor.

"I am thinking of suggesting counselling," said Ross, "What do you think?"

"Well if you want my advice," replied Foster, "There is only one guy who can pull Jack away from his demons, and that's Jack himself. He's had to take more than any man should have to bear, I don't think some shrink emotionally massaging Jack's head is the answer he is looking for to the questions he needs answering. This place gives me the creeps," said Foster.

"Is it the place or the people who do the cutting that scares you?" said Ross smiling.

"Both I guess," he replied. "More so the morbidity of the cutters," Foster winked, smiling back.

"I will let you know if anything else develops," said Doctor Ross, pushing open the door.

"Thanks, I will keep an eye on Jack," he replied, before turning and slowly walking down the corridor.

TEN

Olivia Salmach bore a son in the year 1966; they had been overjoyed at the healthy baby's arrival. Nebi had been sent to Turkey for a meeting arranged by the British government to gather information from a Turkish agent who had links to the KGB. What turned out to be a simple operation, ended with him almost being killed?

He was sent to a safe house in Bursa where he was to meet with the agent, along with a major player within the Russian organisation who had agreed to pass on vital information, and in return he would be allowed to defect to England. The operation was to be a "pass-over" of information that the Russian had to offer, which then was subsequently forwarded on to MI6 for assessment. A few hours work then they would spend a couple of days in Istanbul before flying onto Egypt, as Nebi had wanted his pregnant wife to see the country he was born in. He had recently been given news his ailing mother had taken ill.

For a while Nebi had studied the safe house, which stood at the end of a narrow cobbled lane opposite a small churchyard, a few peasant women shifted around the ancient gravestones like shadows in silence, a breeze whistled across the still air stirring the barking of a small dog.

The shutters were clasped shut upon the face of the house; there was no sign of movement. For a while he waited as the daylight hours began to diminish and the last of the sunlight was swept into the arms of the oncoming dusk.

He approached the side of the house, for a moment he thought he heard a sound from the rear; he walked towards the front door which was opened slightly. Carefully he placed his hand against the door and pushed it inwards as he began to enter. There was an uneasy feeling tingling in the air he could not shake off, that only heightened his senses.

Nebi walked in through the narrow entrance, and could see the outline of the side door leading to a front room on the left. For a moment he stood outside the room, the silence now began to disturb him; he gripped the handle, his teeth clenching as the door creaked as he pushed it open. At first he did not enter the room except reaching inside caressing the side wall until he felt a light switch. He took a deep breath before flicking the switch, and quickly entering the room. The agent he was to meet was sprawled across a small brown leather settee; there was a clean shot to the head and two more to the man's chest. Nebi quickly backed up nervously against the door, pulling his gun from inside his jacket; he scanned the rest of the room before edging his body around the doorway back into the hallway. Nebi noticed his breathing was the only thing he could hear in the unnerving silence within the house. He looked down the passageway towards where the kitchen was situated, this too was in darkness except for the outline of a man sitting still at a table, he walked down noticing that even though the man was sat in an upright position, his head dangled awkwardly over his right shoulder, his throat bore a deep gash as the trail of blood poured freely down his shirt forming a pool across the surface of the table. He blinked against the darkness, for a moment something moved beside the dead man, Nebi could just make out the silhouette of someone crouched beside the edge of the kitchen table then there was a white flash.

Nebi fell back against the floor clasping his leg; a hot searing pain throbbed as he could feel a fine line of blood trickle across his skin.

The figure stood upright firing another shot before fleeing, Nebi fired of two rounds as he began to scramble to his feet. For a moment the sound of sirens seemed to vibrate in the distance, he had to get out of there. He clutched the side of his leg feeling the flowing blood seep into the fabric of his trousers, as he scrambled towards the door; he could hear a car engine roar into life as it screeched across the darkness and sped away. He almost fell out into the narrow side entrance to the house; it was shielded from the front by a row of trees that seemed to over-hang covering the right external side of the building. The sirens were getting louder; he managed to climb over the side wall, adrenalin forcing him to run across a field that led to a dirt road where he left his car out of sight beside a barn, he knew he had been lucky this time.

Through a contact, Nebi had arranged a quick departure from the country via a local airstrip upon a cargo plane; he was not taking any chances, as the obvious departure locations could be watched. The cargo plane was bound for Africa. Without any warning Olivia had begun to show signs of a premature labour once the plane was airborne.

Nebi could only watch as Olivia was about to give birth in Middle Eastern airspace as they flew from southern Turkey across the north tip of Syria through Israel and Jordan, bound for Africa. The birth had gone without complications to the relief of the child's nervous father, who had wept at the first sight of his son. They had been the only passengers on board the small cargo plane, along with a group of Red Cross volunteers who were heading towards the civil war in Nigeria. One of them, an African national named Roweena, and also a qualified nurse had helped with the delivery of the baby.

"He is beautiful," said Roweena, holding the small baby aloft.

"Yes, he truly is," said Nebi as he looked upon the face of his son for the first time. Nebi held his wife's hand. "I love you," he said, carefully wiping her damp brow, which flickered with perspiration.

"I love you," said Olivia smiling, tears rolling down her face.

"Look!" shouted Roweena. "There across the sky," she pointed excitedly towards the glass of the small window.

"It's beautiful," she went on. Nebi crouched down curiously, running his hand across the dull interior of the plane's window, he peered outside, and the dark sky seemed to linger like a slow-flowing black ocean into nothingness, only to be broken by a stream of light that poured across the contours of the plane's exterior illuminating the wings, it was almost as if they could be brought to life, and begin to flap like a giant bird suddenly taking flight across the oblivion of space.

At first Nebi had thought it was flashes of lightning in the distance, as the light seemed to flicker against the darkness.

"What is it?" he asked, placing his hands around his eyes against the glass to get a closer look.

"It's a star," said Roweena. "A bright shining star, it is a good omen, he will be a lucky child," said Roweena, "he will be a great man." Again she held the child aloft; the other Red Cross volunteers gathered around the child and began to pray.

Nebi stared over at his wife, raising his eyes.

"We had better give this great man a name," he said smiling.

"Gabriel... I think we should call him Gabriel," said Olivia.

"Perfect!" said Nebi. "That is a great name for what will be a great man."

Nebi had watched his wife sleeping, the child beside her. He would fight all the dangers in the world to preserve his family's safety, his safety was secondary, yet he could feel the imminent danger that awaited him, he knew the Russians had been tipped off somehow on the meeting at the safe house. He was expected but why? Was there a traitor in the organisation? Or was it just coincidence? He immediately dismissed this thought, he always felt coincidences were always in some way or another orchestrated for a relevant purpose.

He again glanced out of the window, his weary eyes fixed upon the large star as it just flickered in the distance, a lone beacon of light pressed against the vastness of a dark and lonely sky.

ELEVEN

There was a chill that moved around the high altar and across the elevated plane in the sanctuary, which seemed to rasp against the stillness and silence of the church. The candles that burned upon the altar flickered as small flames licked against the air as if dancing into an almost contrived unison. The communion chalice had been tipped on its side; the irregular shape had been crushed, as if forced into an almost strained expression as it lay towards the surface edge. Consecrated wine had seeped across the cloth covering, slowly dripping upon the floor like fine droplets of blood.

Pew seats that ran circular on either side of the sanctuary lay empty, prayer books were stacked neatly at the edge of every second row closest to the outside aisles where elaborate carved Stations of the Cross depicting Christ's final hours, stretched adjacent across each wall. A statue of St Peter stood solemn to the left of the altar, and the Virgin Mary stood to the right, her hands outstretched in a sort of welcome gesture.

A gust of wind blew some unwelcome leaves inside the church, as Sister Agnes pushed the church door open; they hovered in the air before gliding to the ground as she slid the door shut. Her meticulous cleaning trait forced her to kneel down as she hurriedly picked up the damp leaves putting them in her pocket, she could not help feeling the church seemed colder than usual.

"I bet Father Dyer has left the side door open again," she said to herself, shaking her head before reaching towards a stack of hymn books that had toppled over onto the floor.

Sister Agnes had lived in the parish of St Luke's for almost sixty-eight years and had been a member of the nunnery for forty-three of those; she had given herself to God a long time ago. Life sometimes can force you into choices, as your choices force you into the life you lead; the church had been her "protective sanctuary", the life she once new had been a long ago memory and in a way her choice had been forced by a cruel twist of fate. She had known love, and its heartbreak. He had been an RAF pilot during the Second World War, and for a time they had shared a great love. They had made their eager plans for the future; he had been flying back from a captured German airbase in France when his plane went missing over the English Channel, witnesses reported engine failure, as the plane nosedived, smashing amongst the waves, before disappearing into the icy depths of the water.

She had taken the news badly, at first it seeped into her slowly, seemingly taunting her reasoning and understanding as the undercurrent of shock washed over her. That feeling of loss was hard to bear, it went beyond bereavement, until she retreated into her faith, and the embrace of God where she would remain for the rest of her life.

She looked across the rest of the nearby pews but nothing else seemed out of place, yet something did not seem right. For a moment she stopped, a shiver ran across her shoulders as what she saw did not register. Sister Agnes quickly turned around and glanced at the other wall, her eyes widening.

"My goodness," she said, raising her hand towards her mouth. "Who would do such a thing?"

The Stations of the Cross had all been turned upside down, and something dripped across them, oozing down the surface of the walls slowly seeping across the floor, what at first looked like simple red paint splashed across the holy stations by vandals had now become obvious... to be blood.

At first it seemed to move with a mind of its own, in a slow deliberate motion, creeping as it gathered, forming into a pool across the aisles as if it was alive. She was unable to move, all she could do was witness this unnatural phenomenon take place before her eyes.

Towards the altar the candles flickered as if ushered by the sudden chill that had now become more intense. Sister Agnes walked forward at first ignoring the splashes her footsteps made as she moved towards the front of the church, as her intention was focussed on something else in the distance. At the back of the altar the statue of Christ had fallen down and broken into several pieces scattering across the floor. She stood for a moment, her hand still held across her mouth and her face white as the bloodless statues before her. "In God's name who would do such a thing?" again she asked as her mouth quivered. She slowly raised her head above to where the statue of Christ had fallen, and what she witnessed made her legs begin to shake, she could not scream as the contents of her stomach began to make their way up her throat. She gripped the side of a pew as she began to vomit violently across the wooden benches.

She began to breathe in short steady bursts at first refusing to open her eyes, hoping the image had gone away. Sister Agnes slowly raised her head towards the large wooden crucifix, "Oh no... oh my God no." The cross had been turned upside down, and Father Dyer was pinned naked to it. Two thin lines of blood seeped from his eyes across his chest silently dripping down towards where she stood.

Outside, the still night air became littered by faint drops of rain and snow particles that fell side by side in the silence; there was a faint spasm of searing screams that came from within the church that just became overwhelmed into the eerie stillness.

Three hooded figures emerged in monk robes and just stood by the cornerstone of the church, their silhouettes lingered in silence like hovering spectres.

For a while they stood motionless, deathly still as if awaiting some kind of order or command. The tallest of the three figures moved towards the rear where he turned and bowed slightly, Abigail Tripp had stood across the road, her head tilted, and her eyes seemed to blaze against her pale face, as he looked into them he felt their command, their order. This small young girl stood devoid of innocence and the natural feelings a girl this age should possess. Instead, an inherent evil brimmed within her, stirring like bubbling molten lava, that whatever guided her... possessing her... could only control.

TWELVE

Father Creegan turned the small Fiat in through the church gates, the gravel crunched and sprayed around the wheels of the car as it jolted to a stop. For a moment he paused just gripping the steering wheel as he glanced across at the outline of the church, his eyes following the surmounting cross which disappeared into the gloom above, white speckles of snow flickered down against the headlights falling slowly against the wind, cascading hypnotically.

He began to put the last few days' events in rewind within his head as he tried to analyse and pigeon hole his thought complexities, which were jumbled and in disarray like a ransacked room within his disordered mind.

Father Creegan was a rational man, an intelligent man; he still felt concern for Gabriel Salmach, concern about his state of mind. He gripped the crucifix around his neck, holding the cross tightly in his hand before him, again just staring out at the church. There was a faint sound of carol singers in the distance, as the voices of the choir dripped across the air. Another priest would stand in for mass as he had requested.

He sat back in the seat, just studying himself in the mirror. He looked older than his fifty-four years; the lines that ran down the side of his face gave distinction and a certain intensity, like a weathered book cover concealing his histories and thoughts. And although his eyes were heavy-lidded and tired, they were inquisitive eyes, friendly eyes.

He slowly climbed out of the car, the cold night air felt cool against his face as he pulled the collars of the coat up around his neck before retrieving his hat from the passenger seat.

Father Creegan walked across the front of the church grounds towards the rectory unaware he was being watched.

70

He pulled the keys out of a side pocket in his coat as he approached the small house. He stepped onto the wooden porch scraping off several fallen leaves with the edge of his shoe. For a couple of moments he fumbled with the keys struggling with the inadequate glow of the porch light. The figure began to move across the grass towards the priest. He pushed the small brass-coloured key in the lock vigorously turning it until it clicked open. He was about to walk in the door when the figure rushed up behind him, reaching out and clutching his shoulder, the priest quickly turned startled.

"Hello Father," said the tall figure. Father Creegan stepped back, studying the face that appeared forged against the darkness.

"Jack, is that you Jack?" he asked peering out into the dark. "If you're trying to see this old priest off you're going the right way about it," he went on, as he exaggeratingly rubbed the centre of his chest. Bannerman stepped into the light of the porch. He paused for a moment, "Father I need to speak with you," said the detective, not hiding the urgency in his voice. Father Creegan opened the door of the rectory, "I told you I would always be here for you Jack, day or night, come on in." He led Bannerman in to the small hallway; the detective could not help noticing a faint smell of lavender hung in the air, as they walked towards the living room. The priest took the detective's coat hanging it upon the wooden stand at the end of the hall.

"Drink, Jack?" asked the priest running a cloth around the rim of a glass, "I got something stronger than tea." Bannerman nodded, sitting by the open fire. The priest pulled a three-quarter bottle of whisky from a drawer beneath the writing bureau at the side of the window.

"You know Jack," smiled the priest, "behind closed doors this is my one great sin," he said tapping the bottle. "Yet," he went on, raising his eyes, "we kind of have a truce, an understanding. I treat it with respect, and it helps me to sleep." He sat down opposite the detective slowly sipping the whisky. "How have you been Jack?" he asked, for a moment Bannerman stared hard into the fire, ignoring the priest's gaze, the flames flickering across his concerned face.

It had been on the detective's many visits to the church, which had started several months ago, that the priest had come to know him. He would sit through mass then still be there many hours after it had ended, just sitting in silence at the back of the church, seemingly praying, his eyes fixed, just staring ahead. The priest had long sensed an imploring that seemed to have exuded from this man, the helplessness this man had felt had long stirred within the priest's own heart.

Father Creegan had known of Bannerman's troubles, of what had happened to his family. The events leading to his wife's breakdown following the tragic loss of their daughter, which had also led to her subsequent suicide attempts. This had forced Bannerman to have her sectioned within a secure unit for her own safety.

It had not been the first time she had tried to kill herself, but it was on the last occasion that she almost succeeded. Bannerman had tried to be there for his wife, amidst his own grief and loss he never lost sight of how she was affected; her grief was gradual, like the onset of some great tidal wave of despair that was slow in coming, yet the aftermath of its arrival proved devastating.

One evening he walked into the house, the silence seemed uneasy, almost as if it was throbbing in the air. Maybe it was that marital bond, that unity two people share when there is a deep love between them, that had heightened his perception of what he was about to find. He rushed up the stairs where most of the rooms lay in darkness except for the main bathroom. Although the door was closed he could see the light was on inside. He reached for the handle pushing the door, except it had been locked. Bannerman yelled out his wife's name several times before he forced the door open; she lay in the bath as if she was asleep. But the empty bottle of pills that floated in the cold water she lay in had made him come face to face with his worst fears. He had not realised she had already slipped into a coma. The medical unit first on the scene was quick to administer CPR as without oxygen the brain cells will start to die within a few minutes. All he could do was watch helplessly as they performed

72

chest compressions and rescue breathing. It would take several minutes before she was brought back to life.

The oncoming weeks would prove very difficult for Bannerman, as his wife had emerged a different person. It was almost as if she resented him, resented him "bringing her back"; back from a place she could once again be with their child. A place where the pain would cease, sometimes when there is nothing else, a person can emotionally "retreat" backwards within the safe chapters of past memories. She refused to except the loss, as if the reality was distorted, what had happened was an abstraction, a slant on reality that lay as if beneath ripples on water, unclear, continually flurrying, shimmering against the revelation put before her.

Bannerman would watch his wife wither before him both physically and emotionally; if he did not do something he knew his daughter would not be the only loss he would have to endure. For a time his existence was like hovering within the periphery of a nightmare.

"There has been a murder Father," said Bannerman staring intently, his eyes narrowing as he studied the priest.

"Well Jack," replied Father Creegan, placing the palms of his hands against the fire. "You must come up against murder all the time, why has this one brought you here?" Bannerman watched as the priest sat back in his chair. Bannerman took a sip of the whisky, the flames of the fire reflected across the contours of his glass as he held it before him.

"You know Father, whisky and women have long been described as the ruin of a good man." The detective gave a wry smile.

"Well now Jack, I have only really tasted the pleasures of one of those predictable ruins," said the priest gulping down the rest of his drink.

"I have a feeling I may need another for what you are about to tell me," he continued, as he tipped the bottle towards his glass.

"The victim was a priest," said Bannerman, for a moment there was a silence between the two men as if the word "priest" evoked a sudden stark realisation, that even a man of the church is not immune to murder.

"Do we know who he was?" asked Father Creegan standing before the detective.

"That's one of the reasons I am here. We are assuming he is the parish priest of the church where he was found."

"What church?" he asked, stepping forward, placing his glass upon the small side table beside Bannerman.

"The Heritage Church" replied Bannerman, carefully studying the priest. "It's across town, I noticed it's kind of a modern name for such an old building," he went on.

"Why... that's," Father Creegan held his mouth, "Oh my G... I knew this man – it's Father Merrick, do... do you know what happened?"

Bannerman paused for a moment, "All I can say it was not pretty, I would rather spare you the details Father."

The priest slowly shook his head as he slumped back down in his chair, making the sign of the cross. "Good God," he said before gulping down a large mouthful of what was left of the whisky.

"It seems he wasn't that good Father," said Bannerman reaching into his inside pocket.

Father Creegan just looked at the detective frowning.

"I'm sorry," said Bannerman, acknowledging the priest's confusion. "I am referring to your previous comment, when you said your God was good," he continued, "I fail to see how this can be determined?"

Father Creegan just looked at the detective for a moment.

"It is not something you can ever determine by our actions, whether God is good, Jack," he went on.

"Yes I know, Father, but please don't hand me the 'we have free will' speech, as clearly God does not take into consideration our actions, as I tried to live my life honest, and righteous, and now and again would glance in the good book, just trying to do what was right, yet he saw fit to hand my daughter a death sentence."

The detective's features began to tighten.

The priest for a moment just studied Bannerman. "Yes Jack, I am classed as a man of God," he said, "but I do not pretend to have all the answers. There are things that happen in this world that go beyond my understanding, and there are times when I lie awake at night and question my own faith and belief. But Jack," he continued, "where would I be if I just threw in the towel, because something has happened I do not agree with, or like, something that lands in my path and I refuse to walk around, and just stick two fingers up to the church."

"We may as well join the line of people who carry bottles in brown paper bags and commit a slow suicide."

"And Jack," the priest moved forward in his chair. "I don't even pretend to know how hard it must have been to lose a child, but I do know life and death walk hand in hand, as do faith and belief, these things are bestowed upon us, given like the very lives we live, or choose to live, this we can choose. But," he went on, "death is something we cannot dictate unless committed by our own hands; a person's calling may come at anytime or any age. I know their life may seem pointless, many people say to me. 'What was the point of being born? Only to exist yet die so young.' But the important thing is Jack," continued the priest, pointing his forefinger towards the detective. "We have been enriched by their presence, and maybe their existences have somehow planted the seeds for our future, for our choices, and the manner we go on to live our lives. This is when we who are left behind have to find the strength to search deep within ourselves, for our own faith and belief, belief that they are with God in a better place, and faith that one day Jack," the priest paused for a moment, "one day we shall be with them again."

Father Creegan sat back in his chair. "I know it's not an easy thing to digest from a priest, my comments may seem almost predictable, but…" again he pointed his forefinger towards the detective, "it's the best this tired old man of the cloth can offer."

"Well, it's better than your whisky," said Bannerman raising his glass. "It's not easy that's all, one moment you think you're destined for the strawberries and cream side of life, when out of

75

the deep blue, you're dealt something that's hard to walk back from."

"I know Jack, my mother died when I was very young; the safe web she had woven around me seemed to evaporate, leaving me exposed to a world with some very harsh realities."

For a moment the priest's eyes, averted towards the fire, that seemed to expose a long ago grief.

"There is not a day that goes by, when I don't think of my mother," he paused, topping up his glass. "But her existence Jack," he continued, "her existence moulded me to what I am." Bannerman watched as the priest raised his hands, "I don't know if that's a good thing mind you." Again he smiled across at the detective. He placed the glass back on the table crossing his fingers. "All I am trying to say Jack, your daughter's existence and passing will affect every decision and choice you shall make for the rest of your life, I am not saying the hurt or bitterness will go away, it seems that sometimes everything surreal is entangled within a mass of jumbled reason, and when unravelled can become clearer, and in time easier to bear."

For a moment there was a contemplative silence between the two men.

"I know you have the strength Jack," he continued, "and I know you will pull through, and Jack," there was sincerity in the priest's eyes as they narrowed, before moving forward in his chair. "Ashley shall be there at the end of your journey, she will be waiting for you, and her spirit shall never cease to be."

Don't worry Daddy, I do not need to be frightened, God has told me in my dreams.

His daughter's words flickered in his mind, as he again stared hard beyond the flames of the fire, as before him her small round face stared back from amidst the throbbing glow, as he just looked on trance-like.

Bannerman quickly gulped down the rest of his drink before reaching into his pocket, pulling out the small evidence bag that contained the piece of paper he had removed from the dead priest.

"Maybe you can tell me what this means," said Bannerman opening the clear plastic bag. The priest looked on as the detective carefully placed the piece of paper on the side table before him. "He was clutching this." Bannerman slowly unfolded the paper with the nib of his pen. "I need to know what connection it could have." He turned the paper towards the priest, "Is that what I think it is?" asked Father Creegan, grimacing as he read the words. "It's not been to the lab yet, but it appears to have been written in blood," replied Bannerman, nodding at the priest. "Anno Domini," he whispered the words slowly over and over.

"You say this was found on the body?"

"Yes he was clutching it," said Bannerman.

"Anno Domini Nostru Lesu (Jesu) Christi. 'In the year of our Lord Jesus Christ'. These words are Medieval Latin, abbreviated as AD denoting years after the birth of Christ. They are also used as the number of a century or millennium."

The two men sat in silence for a moment. Bannerman moved forward, "Yeah and I do believe we are about to start another millennium in a couple of days time," he said curiously.

"There have been suggestions of the second coming of Christ," said the priest. "This is mentioned in the Bible, although there are different interpretations of how when, and where, it is believed he could return on the start of the coming millennium. But I do not see what the killing of a priest signifies, it does not make sense."

Bannerman shook his head, "So we could have some weird religious sect going around killing priests, offering them up on the eve of the oncoming millennium. Surely this is not the will of God?" said Bannerman, there was a trace of cynicism in his voice.

"Well…" said the priest frowning, "contrary to the belief he will return amidst balls of fire on a chariot, and land upon the Mount of Olives, as it states in Luke, 'The kingdom of God does not come with signs to be observed, or with visible display.' Hey no religious lesson Jack," the priest held up his hands, "but no one knows the hour or time that God will choose to send his son back to earth…" For a moment he hesitated, staring into the fire before continuing, "… Or if he is with us already."

"Why would he have this in his hand?" asked Bannerman, "Is it some kind of warning or clue?"

"Or was it something left by the killer?" asked Father Creegan studying the red lettering.

"We have to consider every possibility, at the moment there is no next of kin, the church where he was found was deserted. Would you identify the body?" asked Bannerman.

Father Creegan bowed his head before answering, "Yes, of course Jack, anything to help." The detective watched as the priest stood up, walking across the room towards a small central display cabinet, he opened the glass door, reaching in and clutching a small gold-rimmed black and white photograph of a young woman holding a child. "You have not changed much," remarked the detective. "Only about fifty years Jack," replied the priest sighing nostalgically. "You know Jack?" he went on, "This picture bears the innocence of another age. It depicts a black and white world a lifetime ago. When I was a child all I could do was marvel at the wonderment around me, staring into a deep well whose bottom revealed an unclear future, a kind of distorted adventure awaited, yet it felt good, that thing we called life."

Bannerman watched as the priest held the picture before him for a few moments, before carefully placing it back inside the cabinet.

"How we now exist in such a dark crimson place, amidst the grip of evil," he said turning to face the detective. "The water in that well becomes clearer as we get older Jack, as does what lies beneath it."

"It only becomes more apparent if we choose to see it," remarked the detective. "The evil and sin has always been there, as long as man has."

"There is someone I would like you to meet," said Father Creegan, drawing the curtains together as he noticed the bottom of the window pane had a frosted appearance. "I think he could be of some help."

Bannerman studied him for a moment, before replying. "Oh! How? Forget the mystics and crystal ball brigade," that same cynicism crept back in his voice. "They usually start crawling out of the wall into the lap of anyone who will give them the time of day, when something like this happens, and believe me they can do more harm than good."

"He is nothing like that," remarked the priest. "However, he did foretell your visit here tonight."

There was a whirring inside Bannerman's inside pocket as his phone began to vibrate. "Excuse me Father, I must take this," he said frowning at the phone as he slid it open.

"What is it sergeant?" he asked walking to the far side of the room. The detective listened in silence before putting the phone back inside his pocket. He turned facing Father Creegan.

"There has been another killing, and it's a priest."

THIRTEEN

Ethan Cole would do his rounds looking in on the various patients checking that they had bedded down for the night. This was not just a routine as he glanced through the glass viewing sections upon the doors of their rooms. It was not something he did before "clocking off". It was something he did because he really did care. He would take time to look upon the faces of the younger patients, as he would be the reassurance against the undeniable fear in their eyes. People would be brought here after tragic accidents where they had lost a limb, or left with the loss or impairment of the ability to move or function, due to partial or complete paralysis.

He knew what it was like to feel helpless, to feel rejection, and most of all feel scared. To be scared within a world that was unknown to them. Some of the patients, whose injuries would be so severe that they would feel a burden to their families and friends, even though this was not the case, would seemingly, react with bitterness and hostility to those who would offer support. The more severe the injury, the more care was needed. They needed empathy and patience, compassion and consideration; Ethan was the go-between to aid them in not only coming to terms with their physical disabilities, but he would also aid them in their psychological recovery. Ethan knew how fragile the human body was, so it was not only the body he would work on to repair. He would reach inside towards their spirit. He knew the body when broken could somehow lose the spirit. And without spirit the body can cease to function, and cease the desire to live.

He stood by the doorway of Ben Mills, who at fourteen years old was one of the youngest patients at St Michael's. Ben had been linked up to a machine for the past nine weeks. The machine was keeping him alive by elective ventilation, a complex process whereby the lungs take in oxygen that the body needs, then gather up and expel the build up of carbon dioxide as a result of body functions.

A plastic tube had been inserted through the mouth into the trachea, this was beneficial in keeping a clean supply of oxygen to his organs, until the machine is finally switched off, after brainstem death, and the organs can be removed for transplantation. As it was only recently he was pronounced brain dead.

On first reading his medical history Ethan had wept. He wept as he looked at the helpless child who just looked as if he was resting in a deep sleep, dreaming what should have been an ordinary fourteen-year-olds innocent dream.

His mother had been a drug addict and was found overdosed on heroin by his younger sister, the two children had been left with their brutal stepfather. Ben had always hated him, the boy had always sensed there was something "about" him, something "not right" and his stepfather reciprocated the boy's perception by severely beating him whenever it took his fancy. As Ben's punishments grew more severe, he would be regularly kept from school until the purple patches to his back, ribs and legs would clear up. His stepfather would offer an inane list of various excuses for the boy's absence, yet the school never became suspicious.

Ben had tried hard to avoid the senseless beatings, yet he knew by taking them his stepfather's attention was on him and not his sister.

He would sit in the silence of his room waiting for the key to slot in the front door, and then the footsteps climbing the stairs often with a stumble or a fall, this signalled his step father's drug-induced and drunken condition. Sometimes he would stand outside his room, the thin shadow that crept across the floor from the bottom of the door, would cause the boy to shake uncontrollably until he would wet himself.

But sometimes his stepfather would walk away towards his sister's room, where he would enter and remain for sometime before leaving. Her stifling cries would burn against his ears, as he himself would weep long into the night.

He would wait before climbing down the stairs in search of food. This existence was endured for many months; sometimes their stepfather would not return for days, and then the fumbling of the key would signal the worst. One night his sister's screams, had become too much. Ben felt something stir within him that was not fear, but hatred, a burning hatred for this man that drove him to snatch at the handle of the cricket bat which lay at the side of his bed.

For a moment the hatred turned into a blinding rage inside the boy as he ran at his stepfather unhesitant, attacking him with what strength he could summon from within his young body. Ben swung the bat at his stepfather's head; it connected with a crisp thud across the top of his scalp. The boy watched, as his legs seemed to wobble before he keeled over onto the floor, a fine line of blood formed across the top of his head, before slowly oozing down his face.

His stepfather tried to get to his feet, Ben raised the bat above his head and was about to strike again, but his stepfather's eyes seemed to roll in his head as he slid back to the floor, it had only been his sister's screams that stopped him from smashing his head to a pulp. He had to get her out of the house.

Ben quickly wrapped her in a blanket and led her to the top of the stairs. He stood just staring at the frightened young girl quivering and wide-eyed before she quickly climbed down, turning beckoning him to follow her. The rage within had not left the boy, he gripped the handle of the bat deciding there was something he had to finish, he would make sure they were rid of him forever. He quickly turned, before the blow sent him crashing against the side of the wall, the bat dropping by his side. A slow lapse of time seemed to turn before him as his surroundings became hazy; the walls appeared to shimmer as if melting in front of him. Ben could feel himself being dragged across the floor and a door slamming against the wall. He was again flung hitting something solid; he thought he could hear water gushing, splashing hard against the side where he lay. He could feel a fervent activity around him, but his vision still felt fuzzy, he thought he could once again hear his sister screaming

82

in the doorway, before the cold water lapped against his face. He momentarily blinked as the water fell down his throat; he coughed and spluttered feeling himself choking as his stepfather's hand gripped the back of his head tightly forcing him against the bottom of the bath tub as it continued to fill. The blurred abstractions became only flashes and struggles, until there was nothing – only darkness.

Ben had all but drowned as his stepfather had held his head under the water for almost five minutes starving him of oxygen; he was still barely alive but had been in a coma ever since. His stepfather would leave no survivors; he dragged the boy's sister back in the house and suffocated her.

Ethan wiped the boy's brow; the buzzing of the machine seemed to whirr annoyingly against the stillness. He looked upon his innocent face, shaking his head at the thought of what Ben had to endure in his short life.

"Sometimes, big guy, they say everything is for a reason, but I'm struggling with this one," he said in a whisper, raising his eyes towards the ceiling. He knew the boy would never awaken, never sit up and smile, but he would give life to three or four people by his organs.

"It still don't feel right, yeah! I know you got plans for him," Ethan continued his conversation with the ceiling as he checked the pipes for blockages. "And who am I to question your will? I'm just an overweight black guy trying to make sense of it that's all." His shoulders shrugged as he dampened the boy's brow again. "Look after him Lord; he sure pulled a short straw in this life." He looked towards the door as his lip began to quiver. He reached towards the floor for a strip of tinsel that had fallen from the small Christmas tree he had brought in from home to put in the boy's room. Ethan smiled rubbing his dampening eyes before blowing into a handkerchief. He looked through the window and thought he could see slight flickers of falling snow, as he peered out into the darkness. For a moment his thoughts drifted, as he pictured a warm living room with Ben sat eagerly at the foot of a large Christmas tree, examining the many parcels with his name on, watched by a loving mother and father.

"Come on Ethan," he whispered to himself, "no one ever said this world was made of sugar-coated candy." A single tear fell down the side of his face. "The big guy knows what he's doing." He wiped his face, "It's just that sometimes, he does it… to the wrong person that's all."

Ethan turned towards the door again looking upon the boy, for the last time. "Sleep tight little guy, give those angels hell."

He quietly left the room.

The night breeze had built up as it whistled against the outside window panes as he walked down the first of two long corridors. Ethan was silent and reflective; his thoughts tumbled in his head like the soft falling snow that had begun to thicken outside, forming against the narrow window ledges, clinging to the ground. He liked snow; it had always reminded him of falling popcorn. He approached the second corridor, although long, it curved in a rounded arch at the end, opening up towards the main entrance where a chill rush of air was ushered in from an open door.

The nurse at the desk waved as she was answering the telephone mouthing "Happy Christmas" to him smiling as she raised her eyes pointing to the green party hat upon her head.

Ethan smiled back, although not in a party mood, he nodded his head, before turning his collars up and walking through the main entrance.

He made his way across the car park towards where his car was; he noticed snowflakes gave a polka-dot effect to the side windows of the vehicle.

Ethan rubbed his hand across the glass of the driver's door feeling the cold ice melt against his fingers. He turned looking up at the room Ben Mills lay in as he blew into his cupped hands, before rubbing them together. He opened the car door, easing himself into the driver's seat.

"Man, I need a bigger ride," he said, clicking the seat back. "Maybe when they see some sense and give you a raise," he smiled shaking his head as he started the engine. Ethan flicked on the wipers that began to sway slowly across the windscreen, he watched as snow gathered at the edges before falling towards the sides of the window. He pictured small mounds of popcorn fluffing and popping before him in his head.

For a few moments he waited as the car heated up, he revved the engine, rubbing the inside of the window with his sleeve. Although there were very few cars in the small car park, there was something at the opposite side that made him peer closer towards the glass. "What the..?" He wound down his side window sticking his head out; the car park was only partially lit. He thought he could see the silhouette of a young girl as his eyes narrowed blinking beyond the falling flakes of snow that had begun to thicken. He pushed open the driver's door and carefully eased himself out standing by the side of the car; slowly he glanced around the car park. Apart from his sudden exhaled bursts of breath, the area was enveloped in silence. There was no movement apart from drip falling snow.

"I need some sleep, I'm starting to see things now," said Ethan shaking his head slowly. He could not help walking across towards the dull light that sprayed out before him, pressing the edges of his collars around his neck rubbing his hands. It was near impossible for anyone to just vanish from this position in the car park, if they were there in the first place, unless they walked past him or flew over the fence. Maybe it had been the darkness and gloom combined with the falling snow. As Ethan looked up at the dark sky distant memories flickered in his mind, "his" Christmas's long gone by when he was a child and the world seemed like one great well-wrapped present waiting to be opened. Yet there was something other than the cold and gloom that made him shudder as he began to retreat, not taking his eyes of the two small footprints embedded in the snow where he stood, as if he awaited them to follow him across the vacant car park.

FOURTEEN

THE VISITATION

He was sure someone had been standing at the side of his bed, the dark figure seemed to shimmer against the hollow light, and had been there for some time, just standing silently, watching him. It could have been an apparition, a spectre ushered in from one of those nightmares he would suffer as a child, and had continued to plague him long into adulthood. His eyes blinked slowly and the figure remained, he felt no malevolent force, there was no evil, just a serene calmness that washed over him, moving across him as if he was almost floating above his bed. He did not know why he felt such an eagerness to reach out, or the anticipation that moved through him in a delirious wave of happiness.

Alfred "gunner" Sykes had no reason to be happy; he was eighty years old and dying of gangrene. He had already had his left leg removed from above the knee due to the complication of necrosis or cell death, which due to the decay of body tissue caused by acute thrombosis that had gradually blocked the blood cells forcing the amputation. And this had begun to move up the other leg shortening the blood supply, causing the remaining limb to blacken from the foot to the base of the shin.

The doctors had tried treatments; the latest one, some posh name called "revascularisation", the restoration of blood flow in the effected organ. Alfred new it had not worked, he had known the intricacies of his own body long enough, and he could feel it, almost as if the gangrene had instilled its own reprisal upon treatment, against the remaining limb.

He also could feel his death was imminent, a lifetime as a heavy smoker and the fact he was a diabetic had not helped. Yet he had been lucky, not like some of the patients in here, some of them were just kids. He had had his life, he had not been paralysed and forced to move around in a wheelchair looking at the world in his youth through the eyes of a cripple.

There were two photographs at the side of his bed. One was his beloved wife Lois who he had lost eight years ago. He would spend hours just staring at her smiling eyes that seemed to light up the old picture, "You're watching over me, I know you are, just like you always done." Alfred smiled; his eyes would soften becoming tearful as the photograph resurrected so many memories of long ago days.

"It won't be long now, my love," he said his hand gripping the side of the frame unsteadily. They had been married fifty-four years and had one son. He breathed heavily as he edged himself up in the bed. The other much older black and white photograph was of a group of young men in military uniform.

"I guess I will be seeing some of you lot soon, eh lads?" His wrinkled features broke into a smile, as slowly he rubbed his weary fingers across the surface of the picture.

For a moment he lay back, he was ready; the room became a hazy mixture of ever occurring "events" of his past. Alfred had been a sergeant in the Second World War, the third battalion Welsh Guards. The soldiers in the photo had been his friends. Many whose young eager faces he looked upon were to be killed in battle, and never came home to the valleys of their beloved Wales. Alfred had been one of the only survivors from his battalion to return home alive, he could never work out if it was their tragic loss, or the guilt he felt at being alive, being allowed to walk back from the "hell" of war that had remained with him throughout his life. "The best friends any man could ever have," he would often tell the black physiotherapist whose name he could never remember, who from time to time would come and sit with him, and just listen. He was born in 1919 in the Welsh town of St Asaph. He took the Kings shilling in 1938 serving in Gibraltar at the outbreak of the Second World War. He would go on to witness the Tunisian and Italian campaigns; he would also witness the landings at Dunkirk. For a moment he thought he could hear what sounded like constant gunfire in the distance; he turned frowning, and these once "familiar" sounds building up louder, until it began to thunder spasmodically, his heart raced in his chest. He was back there! The exploding shells, screaming planes roared overhead, as all around death and destruction swept in, like some great overture introduced to a maximum symphony in this human tragedy.

The strong sea air stirred in his nostrils, as darkness began to fall; some would sleep against the cold sand dunes, while others stood solitary along the beach as soft ripples of waves crept around their feet. They looked for oncoming boats approaching amidst the gloom of the dark and silent ocean. For a moment he stood clutching his collars around his neck as the sea breeze rushed around him, the cold familiarity was overwhelming, the smell, and the taste of his past, the company and unity of his comrades. He could hear the slow movement of the water as it washed up along the sand, the white foamed water cascading across where he stood, he looked down as it would recede slowly among the debris and scattered pieces of equipment only to reveal several dead bodies of soldiers and seaman shifting along the water's edge. And again he stood a lone survivor in what became a desolate graveyard.

He watched as the figure began to approach him, it was the outline of a young man, yet unlike a dream, his awareness was real, he could feel and smell his surroundings, there were familiar noises beyond where he lay, but the room remained hazy. He knew it was not the after-effects of his medication as his last dose was administered several hours ago.

Alfred lay back in his bed and smiled, watching as the figure stood before him, a mild glow emanated forth across the room slowly swirling like the sprinkling of sunlight. He had to be dreaming, or was it the start of his next journey?

"Have you come to take me?" he asked. The figure's outline became apparent as he held out his hand.

At that moment the frailty of his body seemed to shuffle from him, his whole being tingled as if revitalised, and a new resurgence flowed through him, he no longer felt old and weak.

The aches and pains of age had gone. Alfred leaned up, removed the bed clothes and without thinking, swung his legs across the bed onto the floor.

His hands gripped the edge of the mattress, he looked upon the smooth skin upon his outstretched fingers, and he could feel the floor underneath both his feet.

"Come and walk with me."

Alfred just sat there for a moment unable to move; he held out his hand feeling no fear, no pain, only peace.

"Who... who are you?" he asked before slowly standing up. Alfred looked across at the photograph of his wife and felt the need to retrieve it.

"It will be okay, come and walk with me."

Alfred followed the figure as he walked towards the door, as the room and walls just shimmered before him.

They walked for a while as the shimmering surroundings revealed segments of his past, flickering momentarily from one stage of his life to another. Then he was looking upon his mother and father as they stood a short distance away in a beautiful garden whose trees, flowers and shrubs seemed to sparkle and glow like an overspill of colour upon a painting.

They both looked upon him, waving and smiling, the look in their eyes was one of assurance and also of welcome.

Alfred was led forward, the further he went the more his past was revealed. His mother wiping away tears from his eyes as his sledge hit a tree stump which jutted out from a narrow precipice across the edge of a snow-covered hill, this when he was eleven years old.

Alfred smiled at the long forgotten memory.

He watched as a young man when he would take his solitary walks around the green hills of his home. Once again a familiar still breeze ushered across the valley, stirring against his nostrils, evoking still deeper memories of the great thinker he had been, as at that period he contemplated the life he was about to embark.

He turned at the brisk continued shunting noise of the paper mill he had worked, and the chattering and laughter of his friends and fellow workers. He stopped for a while as he remembered the scene vividly, as this had been the week before war had broken out in Europe. Alfred watched as the scene began to shimmer as if dissolving back into a long forgotten verse in his life, he watched the young faces of his friends, many of whom were to die within the first months of conflict.

Again he could hear the slow movement of the water as it stirred.

Creeping in, then slowly receding back across the edge of the beach, he stood amidst countless dead bodies that lay scattered across the sand, as if ushered in from the vast toiling ocean. Alfred remained solitary, forged against the howling still breeze, as he looked upon the familiar dead of his fallen friends. The anger he felt stirred with a great sadness that had never left him, yet he also was thankful for the life he had been given, the life he had been "allowed" to live.

He gazed upon the wooden dance floor, and the glee and laughter in the air held a familiar tone as it filled the even more familiar surroundings of the old dance hall. He wiped away his tears and began to smile. The war had ended and this was a happy time, he stood in wonderment as he watched people dancing and singing, although he felt he was oblivious to them, all except the beautiful young girl who stood at the end of the hall, her head tilted slightly, her familiar smiling eyes looked upon him not just with recognition, and admiration, but there seemed to be a beckoning and for the first time Alfred realised he was no longer the eighty-year-old man, but the handsome young man of his prime.

For a moment they were back in the hospital room; the man clutched Alfred by the arm and smiled, there was a radiance and beauty about him that exuded only goodness and peace. "It is time for you to go," he said pointing towards the light that throbbed against the remaining flickers of the dance hall. Alfred walked on towards Lois who was waiting for him. At first they embraced, they embraced for the life they had before, and for the eternity that awaited them as they walked on ahead.

The nurse had looked upon Alfred Sykes with a bemused curiosity, even with the indifference she felt as she looked upon his corpse, as she dealt with many in her normal working week. She could not help notice how serene, how bright he looked, as if he was smiling as she slowly placed the sheet over his face.

FIFTEEN

Bannerman just looked across at the apex of the church, he watched as the snow drifted down slowly, dripping through the gloom. He watched as it began to gather against the bottom of the ornate cornerstone that stood towards the west of the main entrance. It blew in circles shifting across the road in abstract patterns as it settled.

He clicked the car door open and before he was about to get out he turned towards the priest.

"Father, maybe you had better stay here, I don't want you to..."

The priest held up his hand before Bannerman could finish his sentence.

"I know... knew this man, Jack, he was my friend."

Bannerman nodded before stepping out of the car.

Sergeant Foster walked across towards them. "Jesus Christ, Jack, I have never seen anything like it."

Father Creegan stepped out of the passenger side.

"I... I'm sorry Father," said Foster, shrugging his shoulders embarrassedly, as he acknowledged the priest.

"What have we got?" asked Bannerman.

"You better come see for yourself," replied Foster. The detective inspector could not help notice the look of disbelief in his sergeant's eyes as he shook his head.

They walked across towards the church entrance; Bannerman noticed a car parked towards the corner of the graveyard, two smartly dressed men sat in the front seats just observing.

Several police vehicles surrounded the main entrance as he pushed open the door, the silence was broken by continued sobs, and intermittent wails as Sister Agnes was comforted by a female officer, and a more senior police officer was trying to interview her.

Bannerman stood at the beginning of the centre aisle as his eyes averted to what seemingly looked like a wave of blood splashed across the Stations of the Cross along each side of the church.

"Is there a source for all this blood?" asked Bannerman as he knelt beside the wall running his forefinger against the slimy surface rubbing it with his thumb.

"Forensics seem to be scratching their heads with this one Jack," said Foster.

"What do you mean?" replied Bannerman.

He watched as his sergeant pointed towards the crucifix above the altar.

Father Creegan gasped as he held his hand to his mouth, his eyes closed tight as he just slumped back against the wooden bench. Bannerman in turn just focussed upon the scene before him. He walked further down the aisle, looking above at the large wooden crucifix, which seemingly hung upside down with a naked man pinned against it.

He noticed the bustle of activity stop as the police officers and forensic scientists were just staring up at the crucifix in disbelief; Bannerman noticed a young police officer making the sign of the cross.

"Can somebody please cut him down?" yelled Father Creegan, as he began to rush along the aisle, his face tightening in anger.

Two police officers apprehended the priest as he headed towards the altar. "It's okay," said Bannerman holding up his hand.

"What devil could do such a thing?" asked the priest, clutching the side rail that ran both sides of the altar's entrance.

Bannerman and Sergeant Foster watched as the priest knelt down in silence as he looked upon the broken statue of Christ that lay scattered across the stone floor.

"I have never seen anything like this," said Kate Ross as she walked towards the two detectives. "It must be some kind of ritual killing."

"Anything on the blood?" asked Bannerman.

93

"From preliminary findings it appears to bc from an animal."

"Or animals," replied the detective frowning as he just looked at the Stations of the Cross along both sides of the church.

"How the hell did they get him up there?" said Foster, his eyes averting from the horrific scene above them.

"Can we get some ladders or scaffolding and get this man down," said Bannerman staring at the continued droplets of blood falling in uniformed splashes across the church floor from the body above.

Sister Agnes let out a scream that pierced the stillness as she was helped to her feet as she once again looked upon the body of the priest. They watched as she was led towards an awaiting ambulance.

Bannerman walked towards Father Creegan who was knelt praying against the rail of the altar, his eyes closed, as he continually made the sign of the cross with his right hand as he just stared in silence towards the crucifix above.

"Excuse me Father," said the detective as he knelt beside the priest, "I was wondering if there is anything you may know that signifies why the crucifix and Stations of the Cross were left in this way?"

"Only a devil could do this," replied the priest shaking his head.

"There are many interpretations of the upside-down cross," said a voice rasping across the air from the rear of the church. Bannerman turned; watching the small foreign-looking man as he quickly approached up the centre aisle, flanked by two burly guards, the peculiar wide-brimmed hat, the galero that gave the man an air of officialdom looked out of place on top of his head. The detective noticed the guards were the same two men who were sat in the car watching him as he entered the church.

"I am Cardinal Emilio Calvi," announced the man as he gestured the two guards to wait as he approached the detective. The two men stopped, standing erect like bulbous bookends not taking their eyes off the cardinal.

"Your eminence," said Father Creegan as he rose to his feet before kneeling on one knee and kissed the cardinal's hand in respect of his position. "I am Father Jonathan Creegan; this is Jack Bannerman, who is leading the investigation."

"Sir... err, Cardinal," said Bannerman. "This is the second killing we know of and nothing has been released to the press, how have you come to be here?"

A smile broke across the cardinal's face, but his eyes showed no emotion, except for flickers of irritation as he studied the detective, which in turn seemed to breeze between the two men.

"I have come from the Vatican in Rome, and to be brief, I am in charge of an independent organisation within the church, that shall we say," he paused, looking above towards the crucifix, before continuing, "oversee delicate situations like this."

"Delicate situations," retorted Bannerman, pointing towards the dead priest, shaking his head. "You were saying about the cross?"

"Yes, there are different interpretations regarding this act, you see Satanists have been reported to use this form of the Latin cross in their rituals. Or another theory," he continued, "is the St Peter's cross, a Latin cross turned upside down after Peter, who was a disciple of the Christ, who is believed to have been crucified on an upside-down cross so not to be distinguished by the aforementioned Christ." Bannerman watched as he gestured towards the cross above; the detective could not help but feel indifference in this man's demeanour.

"So what I am trying to say," continued the cardinal smiling, "It is a denunciation of the Christian belief." He walked around the altar studying the area, only stopping to survey the crushed communion chalice.

Bannerman walked towards the cardinal, "This organisation you speak of, you do realise this is a police matter?"

"Of course," replied the cardinal, "part of the Vatican has what is called the Roman Curia, which is the administrative apparatus of the Holy See, the central governing body of the entire Roman Catholic Church."

Bannerman frowned at the cardinal and for a moment just stood in silence.

"Excuse my ignorance, sir, but..."

"The Holy See is the Episcopal jurisdiction of the entire Catholic church," interrupted the cardinal.

"What he is saying," whispered Father Creegan, "is that the Holy See is recognised as a sovereign entity, headed by the Pope, in which diplomatic relations can be maintained."

Bannerman looked across at Cardinal Calvi sensing the implications of his comments, and he knew full cooperation would be expected if not forced upon him by his superiors. The last thing the Met. Needed or wanted was a public relations issue with the church. The detective knew that religion could force a stranglehold on anything, however much he rebelled against it; he knew it loomed at the forefront of every major issue in society, was as powerful as any army, and remained the fundamental cause for wars and slaughter that are just as prevalent today as it was centuries ago. But there was something else that made him feel uneasy, something that the cardinal possessed other than his faith; he could feel his undercurrent of influence and power somehow seemed to surpass what he stood for.

However, Bannerman knew he would have to tread softly, these recent events would require sensitivity, and the random killing of priests could stir a frenzy of speculation if these "circumstances" were leaked to the press. Yet the one thing he would be insistent on, that there would be no restraint upon his investigation.

They watched as several uniformed officers brought in two sets of aluminium ladders, as they proceeded to erect them against each side of the cross. A forensic officer was on standby to examine the body before it could be moved.

"Do you have a theory on the blood and the Stations of the Cross?" asked Bannerman as he pointed to the sides of the church.

"Once again whoever did this was trying to emphasise the denunciation of Christian belief; the blood symbolises ritual slaughter."

"So it could be Satanists?" asked the detective.

"Not necessarily," replied Cardinal Calvi. "You see, there are many occurrences of animals being killed, slaughtered, and ritualistically abused for the God portrayed in the Bible, and particularly in the Old Testament."

"I don't follow," said Bannerman frowning, "so it could be Christians?"

"Unfortunately, that is your job Mr Bannerman," said the cardinal scrutinising the detective.

"Forgive me sir," said Bannerman, "but how did you know of these events, like I said there has been nothing in the press?"

The detective walked across to where the cardinal was stood; he noticed the two guards shuffle slightly, as they moved up the aisle towards the end of the pews to the left of the altar, near to where the cardinal was standing before the Eucharist.

Cardinal Calvi turned to face the detective, his eyes narrowing as he felt Bannerman's inquisitiveness.

"May I ask if there was anything either found or written upon the first body?" The detective could feel the probing glare of the cardinal as if he already knew what the answer would be.

"No sir, there was not, although tests are still going on upon the body itself." The detective would keep the evidence to himself for the time being. He ignored Father Creegan's glare as he acknowledged the lie, but had remained silent.

"I see," said the cardinal smiling, looking upon the detective as if he was subconsciously peeling the skin of his lie.

"May I be frank with you?" said the cardinal clutching the detective's forearm and leading him towards the back of the altar. He turned facing Bannerman, pausing for a moment, "These are not just murders or rituals of some deranged cult, you must understand and believe the seriousness of these events, which have followed a chain of sequences like a domino effect whose motion has been irreversibly set." Again he paused before continuing, "I am part of an organisation that stretches across the world, with people in positions you would find hard to comprehend, and believe are an integral part of its existence and continuity."

Cardinal Calvi sensed Bannerman's confusion anticipating his questions, as he held up his hand. "I am aware of hearsay and conjecture; this is in some way a naivety upheld that only caresses the surface of what is the truth, and what is to be very real." The cardinal again smiled at the detective, his grip tightening on Bannerman's arm. "But let me tell you, we exist amidst the periphery of conjecture and hearsay, we are real, Mr Bannerman." His grip loosened as he looked up at the crucifix, and the naked priest. "This is only the beginning."

He looked hard at the detective.

"This is the second murder within the last twenty-four hours, am I not right?" asked the cardinal raising his eyes.

Bannerman nodded.

"Well this is the eleventh priest to have been killed; I cannot stress how important your honesty is."

The detective's eyes widened as he looked upon the small Italian cardinal, "Eleven!" Bannerman shook his head, "But... but what is the significance? And why kill priests?"

"The priests signify the Apostles of the Lord, or the twelve men who were the original followers of Jesus Christ. You see, the original twelve men had received a mission from God," continued the cardinal. "The 'seliah' from the Aramaic tongue referred to those despatched by the mother city, would stand upon the path and welcome the coming of the Lord as he enters the world as the imperishable, glorious and immortal Christ, as it is stated will condemn the 'Diabolos' or Devil to the lake of fire, or the abyss, where he will remain for a thousand years until the God should determine to release him."

The cardinal paused before continuing, "It is stated that the 'epiphany' will be public and glorious, but! We do know the Christ was reborn in human form upon this earth, we know Mr Bannerman that the Christ is already here, and he lives among us, and is yet unaware of whom he really is."

Bannerman studied the cardinal before looking across at Father Creegan who remained silent. The detective looked around the church at the scene before him; what the cardinal was saying stirred within the confines of his rationality, of what made sense to him.

He dealt in fact, on what he could see; this seemed like some religious fruitcake whose inept ranting found solace only in those of equal absurdity.

Normally his common sense would dismiss such a ridiculous and incredible statement, but his "misgivings" were structured upon this coming from a cardinal.

What the cardinal had said had left him with an overwhelming sense of both fear and curiosity, surely the obvious explanation would be a simple serial killer, just another run-of-the-mill nutcase who just wanted to soak his deranged hands and stir the dark waters of infamy for his own ends.

Yet within the cold eyes of this cardinal standing before him, he could sense a ripple of fear that lay deep within this man's demeanour, like a frost setting.

"I found this on the other body," said Bannerman, as he reached into his pocket pulling out the plastic evidence bag. "It was words seemingly written in the priest's own blood, ANNO DOMINI."

"There were two of these priest's found slaughtered within the Vatican, one in southern Spain, three in North America, one in the holy city of Jerusalem, one in Stockholm, one in New Mexico, and these two here in England. The words mean, in the year of our Lord Jesus Christ."

"Yeah and the way these men are killed, another denunciation of Christianity," said Bannerman frowning at the cardinal. The cardinal remained silent.

"But what is the connection to the killings apart from them being priests?" asked Bannerman.

"They had all been groomed from birth, chosen as complete religious purity and being, their purpose was to line the path upon the second coming of the Christ."

The detective stood back. "Look Cardinal! With the greatest respect, this is a lot to try and swallow; I am just a simple police officer. I deal with day-to-day occurrences, crimes of varying seriousness, committed by career criminals, robberies, violence and murder I have seen them all Cardinal, witnessed all types of the bad we do to each other, and..." he continued, "most of the time there is reason and motive, these types of crimes are predictable, and they will happen again and again and I will strive to solve them. Although..." he continued, "the varying amounts of evil we do to each other, well..." he paused. "There is some rationality about it, a predictability that we shall commit these crimes, and this is something I understand, something I can deal with, but what you are saying is well..." Bannerman held up his hands.

"I understand you deal with the banality of everyday human endeavours to commit sin, their sordid predictability I would assume is both annoying and amusing," the cardinal smiled broadly. "I also understand your reservations towards the church, but believe me; time is running out, the Devil also walks upon this world and if he succeeds in his aim in killing the Christ before the eve of this coming millennium, while he still remains flesh and blood..."

"So what you're saying is Christ can be killed?" asked Bannerman.

"He feels as we feel, he hurts as we do, while he walks the earth as a mortal he is susceptible to the evil that searches for him."

"Maybe in some way, Mr Bannerman we can repay our sins by protecting the Son of God."

Bannerman raised his eyes.

"And what do we know of this Devil?"

"Like the Christ he can be anybody, any age or gender," replied the cardinal.

"And have we anything to go on?" the detective was struggling to keep his patience in check, here he was in the midst of two horrific murders and he was discussing the existence of the Devil and Jesus Christ.

"We have looked all over the world for the Devil as we have the Christ; members of our organisation have covered every continent upon this planet." Again the cardinal smiled broadly.

"We have anticipated the time of birth, and whereabouts, but as the Christ was born unto man, unaware of whom he really is, well…" he continued, "you can only imagine the extent of our search."

"Any creed or colour," said Bannerman. "And what is more," he continued, raising his eyes again at the cardinal, "this man is without a true identity to himself, he is unaware of what he really is – seems like God threw a wild card into this sorry equation."

"As I said," replied Cardinal Calvi, "he was born unto man."

"You said there were twelve?" continued Bannerman, "twelve Apostles, but only eleven were killed."

"Yes you are correct, Mr Bannerman, there are twelve indeed."

Bannerman and Father Creegan watched as the cardinal walked towards the edge of the altar. "By the end of the week a new millennium shall begin," he continued, "a manifestation to the rule of Jesus Christ, a rule of righteousness and peace."

"By the end of the week the Christ must choose the twelfth Apostle to line the path, upon his return, and let me tell you Detective," said the cardinal raising his voice slightly. "The evil will stop at nothing in its pursuits and goals, and it cannot and will not fail, as the reign of the Christ will prevail and immobilise the 'Diabolos' as this final Apostle must be brought forth upon the eve of the millennium, to be blessed and cleansed and await the coming."

"But surely, your eminence," said Father Creegan, "this twelfth 'Apostle' would be living under a death sentence even before he is chosen?"

"He is protected by the Christ," replied the cardinal, placing his hand upon the priest's shoulder. "Yet we must work together and protect this candidate, you must work with the church, Detective, and find the Christ together."

Kate Ross walked over towards Bannerman, "Jack I have a report to fill out, the initial findings on the first body was nil, now this…" The detective nodded knowingly.

"I need more time to grasp what this meant."

101

"We have found the same thing on all the other priests, and some these words have been literally torn into their bodies," said the cardinal.

"Is it some kind of message or warning?" asked Father Creegan, "We know they mean in the year of our Lord, and we are at the dawn of the coming millennium."

"Yeah," said Bannerman, "maybe it's someone's way of saying this supposed second coming is not going to happen, the killer's way of how do you put it Cardinal? Denouncing Christianity."

A forensic scientist walked across to where they stood whispering towards Kate Ross. "We are ready to move the body," she announced. "It's pinned to the cross which they have managed to dislodge, they are about to lower the whole thing."

They watched as two thick lengths of rope were tied around the sides of the cross and connected to a makeshift winch, which was then tied around the large wooden beams that ran across the underside of the ceiling. The beams had supported the heavy cross; as it was dislodged the apex leaned to one side as it was slowly lowered.

They had threaded the rope across the beams on pulley supports as the cross swayed precariously causing the dead priest's left arm to fall against his body dangling loosely at the side, as if it was eerily waving at the gathering below, droplets of blood dripped from the open wound on the palm, spraying across the pews and backrests.

The cross was lowered in silence; Bannerman looked upon the contorted features of the dead priest, his sightless glare looked back on the world, two fine streams of blood oozed down his face, it was a look that would remain with Bannerman and his colleagues for some time.

The cross was carefully placed against the floor, as forensic officers quickly got to work in examining the body.

There was a taste in Father Creegan's mouth that made him for a moment feel light-headed, he felt the slight swirling in the pit of his stomach begin to rise. Sergeant Foster gripped him by the forearm, "You okay Father?" he asked; the priest nodded unconvincingly.

"Jack, you better come and look at this," said Kate Ross kneeling beside the body. Bannerman and Sergeant Foster walked across towards the forensic team; the priest had been nailed to the cross, and although one of his arms had worked free as the cross had been moved, the point of the nail still protruded through the back of his hand.

"Take a look at this," said Doctor Ross as she slowly turned the hand showing the palm. Blood still oozed freely across the hand from the open wound, yet there was something else, something that looked like the beginning of a word. Bannerman knelt down besides her peering at the dead man's hand. He could see the lettering torn across his palms AN-; Kate Ross carefully dabbed the palm soaking up the free flowing blood revealing more lettering, NO- "It's the same ANNO DOMINI; it's been written across both palms," said Foster shaking his head. Cardinal Calvi knelt beside the dead man and made the figure of the cross against the priest's forehead and began whispering in prayer.

"There is someone I think you should meet," said Father Creegan. "I think... well, I am not sure," the priest hesitated for a moment. "But I think he could be connected in some way."

"Who is this man?" asked the cardinal, quickly rising to his feet, and walking across towards the priest.

"Well, he's a patient in a hospital... he is paralysed." He seemed hesitant in saying the word paralysed.

"Paralysed?" said Bannerman. "Look, I am sorry gentlemen, but this has all the footprints of a serial killer, who has a major, hang up on religion, especially priests. Or maybe there is more than one," he continued, "working within a time constraint depicting the number of the Apostles in some sick killing frenzy before this coming millennium, to create some weird historical murderous statement, for their own ends."

"I wish it was as simple as that," said Cardinal Calvi, walking across towards the last Station of the Cross, he watched as trickles of blood oozed slowly down the wall.

"His name is Gabriel Salmach," said Father Creegan, "I... I just feel we must go and talk with him, before what you said your eminence, I thought he was becoming delusional, but he spoke in what I can only describe as a knowing way."

"Knowing way?" replied the cardinal, turning around, his eyes narrowing as he observed the priest.

"Yes, I do not know how else to describe it, from how I first witnessed him, he... well seemed changed, he spoke at first as if he had found God, and I was pleased, as if he had been enlightened somehow."

For a moment they just stood in silence.

"Okay," said Bannerman, "we need to start the investigation somewhere," he said nodding at Sergeant Foster.

They watched as the cardinal turned without saying a word rushing down the aisle followed by his two bodyguards.

Bannerman walked across towards several uniformed officers, "I want this church covered from top to bottom, inside and out."

"We are ready to take the body," said Kate Ross. Bannerman nodded, "Keep me up to date if you find anything else."

"It's a weird one Jack," said Foster. "We are going to struggle keeping this out of the press."

"Yeah," said Bannerman, as he studied the church, "A weird one it sure is, and I don't like it, I have a bad feeling about this one."

SIXTEEN

That day long ago in the ancient church of Ravello, Nebi Salmach had chosen never to commit another murder. He had continued to work low key for the government, mainly assisting in surveillance operations in England and overseas for the foreign section of the secret service bureau.

This section of the government was largely funded by the Foreign Office, which during the Second World War had been under the supervision of the department of military operations. Now, amidst the turbulent worldwide ripples of the cold war and changing government requirements meant the bureau had to reorient itself, as the threat presented by the Warsaw Pact and the continuing rivalry dominated by the East-West tension brought about by a divided Europe.

That day as he slowly walked back into the sunlight, he had changed. The old church where the mark had sought sanctuary, and knelt down and prayed, his faith was strong, he had prayed to God and in turn survived his assassin. There had been something about the young man who had stood before him, why had a government organisation wanted him dead? When he had appeared to be a man of God, and what he said had been puzzling. "Like me you are a servant of God, it is just that you are still unaware, and like me you yearn for answers." Inwardly Nebi had envied this man's faith, which he felt even in the face of death, had been strong. It had been almost as if his death was unimportant, secondary to what he believed.

For the first time he had felt a deep calm, unlike anything else as he knelt in the silence of the decrepit church, almost as if he had been reawakened, and the realisation seemed to pour over him, as he stood within all that seemed to be right at that moment, opening his eyes to what he had moved so far away from. For the first time in his life he possessed reason and belief.

He had prayed hard that day, he would pray that the Lord would help him to change what he had become, and for giving him the chance to be what he could be.

During that day in the sun Nebi's life was in a way redirected, there was only one path he would walk and it would be a righteous one. Amidst the dilemmas he faced, and the choices he had to make, unfortunately these choices would eventually cost him his life.

He had been posted for a while in Austria, towards the frontier borders south of the Danube towards the Czech Republic and Slovenia, through the hill country that ran across the eastern rim.

Nebi had marvelled at the majestic scenery of the Otztaler Alps near the borders with Switzerland and Italy. This vast central mountain chain, the Tauern, included some of the highest peaks that sat almost dreamlike against the Austrian skyline. On either side of the Tauern that is separated by deep river valleys, whose streams fed by snowfields and glaciers, lay two younger rugged limestone ranges.

The mountains would gradually fall away into the Danube valley in the north, and towards the Vienna basin in the east. Vineyards ran along the valley slopes, winding and curving, opening up towards the forested hills north of the Danube. This became more mountainous as it fell into a wider expanse against the backdrop of permanent snow cover, spilling across the peaks, forming glacial ice sheets that spread out from under its own weight.

Nebi and his family had been constantly on the move, and for the first time in years he had finally felt settled. This magnificent country had not only become their base, but their home.

They had settled just outside the city of Villach in southern Austria on the river Drava that stretched across the eastern foot of the Villach Alps, west of Klagenfurt, and bordering Italy.

The town hall along with the church was a notable landmark which had been rebuilt after its destruction in the Second World

War. This was where Nebi would liaise with various secret service agents in the small municipal office at the rear of the building. He had been told to "sit on" an individual, an inside euphemism for observing a mark. This particular mark was one Maxim Wessler, a German war criminal and dangerous ex-Nazi who it had been rumoured was head of a small organisational infrastructure within the Austrian government. This underlying base was thought to be the supporting pillar of a deviant society of Nazi sympathisers or so it was rumoured. But as Nebi would find out the organisation was something far more sinister than the resurrection of this evil regime.

Nebi had watched Wessler for several weeks; he was a fat balding man with round spectacles that sat at the edge of his nose like some innocent toymaker. He had a friendly face with slightly bulbous red cheeks that seemed to shine against his pale childlike skin, almost as if he had been doused in porcelain enamel. Yet behind his friendly exterior were two round dark eyes that missed nothing.

He would walk his grandchildren to school like any other parent. And he would attend the Church of St Jacob's. Wessler was a prosperous man. He had built up a successful wood product business distributing throughout the country, and providing much needed employment within the local area. Nebi had studied this man who was well liked and loved by his family.

Wessler was generous if not devious; he would contribute to local causes, as he had strong links to powerful government officials and the local police force.

On reading this man's file, Nebi had been allowed to look into Wessler's past revealing a dark side to this elderly generous businessman.

He was born in Berchtesgaden, a town in the Bavarian Alps of Germany, in 1904; the town lay in a deep valley, surrounded almost by Austrian territory.

In later years he would glance upon the place of his birth from the chalets and air-raid shelters of Hitler and Göring, along with other high-ranking Nazi officers, which were situated on the Obersalzberg peak overlooking the town.

During the war he had been placed in charge of the transportation of Jews to any of the various death camps. Maxim Wessler the SS-Oberstumfuhrer took pleasure in leading woman and children into the vast shower rooms. The showerheads were disguised and also designed to emit poisonous gas, made from cyanide crystals known as Zylon B. The stench of death was like a stimulus, he relished the fear in their faces at the realisation of their fate, the screams and pleading stirred his curiosity, he would make notes. He took great pleasure in watching the children suffocate in slow agonising deaths; after all, this was just human vermin, worse than the rats that would gnaw at their bodies before they were burned in the vast pits the Jews had been forced to dig as their makeshift graves. Wessler would prove both efficient and methodical in these tasks.

On the rare occasion anybody was still alive in the gas chambers, he would insist on shooting them whatever their age or gender.

He noted how long it would take people to die in these tomb-like death chambers. His analytical perception would tell him from the expulsion of gas to the burning of the bodies the cost effect of killing as many Jews as possible on any given day. They would be crammed as tight as possible to be more efficient and quicker in the mass murder of these innocent people. And when it was full to capacity those who could not fit in were shot in cold blood where they stood.

Nebi would walk with his young son up the two hundred and thirty-nine steps of St Jacob's, towards the bell tower; this was interlinked with the church only by an arched gateway.

The church stood on a terrace above the end of Villach across from the main square. The boy and his father marvelled at the wonderful baroque canopied altar, above hung a large Gothic crucifix that dated from the 1500s, and towards the choir hung a fresco of St Christopher, this seemed to swirl and glow against the backdrop of the church interior.

Nebi would watch his son caress the stone pulpit; the boy would bow before the altar whispering in prayer as he knelt in the flowing sun that would stream across the church floor as it sprayed through the ornate windows above. Maybe he would become a priest, thought Nebi, as he looked upon the boy with pride.

Nebi would look from the tower that was the perfect position to survey the whole town and surrounding area using zoom-lens binoculars. He watched as Wessler went about his daily business, he and other town hall officials would drive north out of town the same time every day. He followed the dark-coloured Mercedes-Benz as it weaved swiftly through the side roads towards the outskirts of the surrounding Tyrolean landscape; the constant rainfall gave lushness to the countryside as it was not unusual to get rainfall for several days at a time. Nebi knew he would have to find this location.

He turned the binoculars, slowly scanning the town; he looked down surveying the ancient graveyard, whose elegant carved gravestones at the side of the church were occupied by generations of nobility and aristocracy. Nebi had an unusual preoccupation with graveyards, he found them fascinating from being a young boy, this had not been in a macabre way, it was just the peace and serenity evoking certain calm in him, and in some way he relished the spirits' eternal rest, the mundane rigours of the living existence are washed away to eternal peace.

He had pictured these "royal spirits" lingering around the graves at nightfall, in ball gowns and tuxedos, this perpetual gathering continuing night after night in their silent eerie grandeur.

He continued to slowly scan the streets and houses, across the old town square, amidst the people gathering at the town hall. Nebi scanned the fronts of the various buildings and surrounding area. He quickly pulled away from the binoculars peering intently as if his normal vision would enhance what suddenly disturbed him. He peered again through the binoculars and they confirmed what he had seen the first time: that somebody was observing him.

SEVENTEEN

THE SECOND VISITATION

Darkness can be forever, endless as it swirls across one void into another; infinite in its extreme, immeasurable by time and space, moving along vast chambers of silence with each end only met by a new beginning. Ben Mills floated within this endless night, as if he were suspended in some perpetual limbo awaiting the first flickers of a dawn that would never come.

Maybe for a brief time the body hangs on forcing the spirit to remain, as somewhere within, our hope and faith which we have offered up belies the answers that elude us in life. The spirit rises up in anticipation; for within our brief lives, all that we have endured, and all that we have prayed for in our living existence is now like a journey at an end. As the final revelation to what lies ahead as we move towards the journey into our afterlife.

There were faint flickers of light, very slight at first then the feeling of movement as vibrations began to trickle from within. A still breeze brushed against him, the lights seemed to blink in the distance, continually like sparks fizzling against the void, yet still so far away. The movement became stronger, as if he was being pulled slowly across these vast plains of infinity.

For a while the movement continued, the light continued spasmodically beating with the rhythm of a faint heartbeat. The light stretched into streams, vast lines forming openings across these eternal dark curtains.

"Awaken Ben." The voice crisp, as it moved across the darkness, in a flurry that trickled around him like cool flowing water, as if submerged in the words.

The voice continued, "Awaken Ben."

Ben Mills had been pronounced brain dead, hooked up to a man-made connection that kept the body lingering within the periphery of existence. Now slowly with the spoken words that commanded him, the vibrations of life gradually began to trickle through him.

Ben began to stir, moving slowly, he turned his head from side to side as his eyes moved in rapid unison before opening. He continued to turn his head blinking away the blurred abstractions that lingered before him.

His hands tingled as his fingers outstretched, he began pulling at the wires and tubes, retching and heaving against the tube that ran down his throat. Ben began to pull it out of his mouth, he vomited, coughing hard. The alarm began to sound on the machine in a continuous beeping noise as he continued to shrug and pull at the various wires that had hooked him up to it. Memories flashed against the darkness amidst the silhouetted shapes around the room as his eyes were trying to focus on what shimmered before him.

Ben experienced faint flashes that made him shudder and uncomfortable, he knew something bad had happened. Images continued to come fragmented and broken, as slowly his mind would put them together. He remembered the water as his head was thrust into the coldness. His sister's face loomed before him, her eyes wide. He could almost caress the fear instilled within them as he looked beyond; the images began to reveal the final moments before the darkness would come.

"Ben, come and walk with me," said the voice that softly trailed across the air before him.

The boy felt a calmness and peace as he was compelled to just listen to the spoken words that came from across the other side of the room.

He blinked continually as he looked upon the figure standing at the bottom of his bed, and he began to shake; yet he felt no fear, the bright stream of light fell across the boy's face as he held up his hand against his eyes. He remembered his stepfather, he remembered how he had stood before him, and once again he could taste the hatred he had for this man.

Ben watched as the figure stood emanating streams of light across the room, caressing the walls and ceiling. He began to move anxiously as he looked around for his sister. Yet his eyes turned towards the figure before him, drawn towards this strange apparition that evoked a serenity and calmness that felt good.

The light sprayed more intensely as it moved beyond the walls, as they began to shimmer as if dissolving around him. The boy remained confused yet calm as he witnessed the wonderment before him.

Ben had not realised he had lingered between life and death for several months. The figure walked across towards him and held out his hand smiling.

"Come and walk with me Ben," he said again.

The boy edged out of the bed unsteadily placing his feet upon the floor before slowly standing up. For a moment he stood within the room he had laid for months as he walked towards the man. They walked into the centre of the light. The confused boy thought he was wandering in the midst of a dream; Ben would often dream, usually vivid and dark, never happy, as there was never anything to be happy about within his life. These dreams although suppressed, would remain within his subconscious boundaries, flowing slow and deliberate like a deep dark river, containing all the bad memories that were submerged within him physiologically.

The compulsion to walk with this man was strong, to follow him felt right and it held no fear for the boy.

As he looked upon the man, Ben noticed he had a kind face with strong clear eyes; the eyes could be described as intoxicating as if they held the full colour of all the oceans upon the world, and there was an intensity and kindness within their glare.

Ben watched as they walked on ahead and the room appeared to just fall away like a crumpled piece of wrapping paper. They continued to walk on when the boy stopped abruptly, peering ahead in the short distance where there was something he recognised. It was his Aunt Hazel, Ben smiled. Hazel had been his mother's elder sister and he had always loved her more than his own parents; he noticed she wore her favourite powder-blue dress, that looked like white lilies had been painted all over it, with a frilly v-neck collar and matching hemline. Aunt Hazel smiled at him and waved.

Ben smiled back and waved furiously, maybe this was a happy dream, maybe this dream would never end and he could stay within it forever with his beloved aunt. Ben had been just old enough to remember his aunt dying; the disease came very quickly.

"There is something inside me Ben, something that will take me to God, and this will happen very soon. You will have to be strong, not only for yourself but your sister. I am sorry for leaving you Ben, but God is with us, you must always remember that."

He had sat by her bed, clutching her frail hand refusing to leave until she fell into the long sleep, but before she died she promised him she would see him again, "Have faith Ben." In some way she would be always there for him, as he was the son she never had, the son her sister had not deserved.

For a while Ben stood still just looking upon his aunt, until he noticed something moving in the foreground, walking slowly towards Aunt Hazel, it was his sister.

His sister smiled at him waving slowly, yet there seemed a touch of sadness in her eyes, perhaps it was because she knew Ben could not stay within the place she was. Ben had pulled away from the man's grasp and began to cry; he tried to walk towards them but the more he walked, the distance just stayed the same. He held out his hand as if yearning their touch, their embrace. But he somehow had a self-awareness that he had reached the point he could not go beyond.

"I wish to be with my sister and aunt," he said turning towards the man. "I want to go with them."

"For all that you see before you Ben," said the man, out-stretching his arm. "And for all those, whom you have loved in life, shall share with you in abundance what lies before you, in eternity. But that shall be another time," he continued. "You have to return, and fulfil your purpose."

Ben looked upon the face of this stranger, this man who smiled down at him warmly, whose outline seemed to hang against the light that just pulsated and oozed beyond where he stood. He turned to face his aunt and sister, who both waved towards him, trickles of tears had begun to roll down his face, as he just smiled back waving at them. For the first time he felt that this had been more than a beautiful dream, his instincts had told him it was real, so real that he knew he would return one day, he was only a young boy, as the assurance he felt was overwhelming, yet he felt as if he was stood outside everything that was real and made sense, he knew that he had been taken to a place where there would be no hurt or pain. The look in his aunt's eyes had told him this. Ben watched as his sister and aunt turned and began to walk back towards where the light was stronger, his sister turned her head smiling, her right hand waving, he had been sure he had seen tears twinkle in her eyes, but they were no longer sad eyes, no longer eyes that held fear and pity for them both.

"Come Ben we must go," said the man turning towards what seemed like a pathway where the light thinned, and Ben could see flickers of the world he was about to return to.

EIGHTEEN

A recent delegation from the Arab league had visited Israel, as plans had been drawn up and a proposal had been offered calling for a comprehensive regional settlement led by foreign ministers from Egypt and Jordan.

The proposal was also for a full recognition of Israel by the Arab and Islamic world. This ongoing divide by Palestine and Israel had resolved around the fate of the West Bank, Gaza strip and the occupation of East Jerusalem by Israel since 1967.

Israel is a small populous state that was established as a Jewish homeland in Palestine in 1948. For many centuries its people have been scattered all over the world, wandering nomadic, not belonging anywhere yet it is felt the Jews have a historical binding to the region dating back thousands of years. This ancient binding is felt no less by the Palestinian Arabs, and a hostility had existed between neighbouring Arab countries ever since.

Since the United Nations partitioned Palestine in 1948 declaring the Jewish state of Israel there has been continued conflict with its Arab neighbours.

Although in recent years these conflicts have ended with land gains by Israel – the Gaza strip, the West Bank of the river Jordan with East Jerusalem, and the Golan Heights across the Syrian border.

It was as if fate had somehow orchestrated Israel's geographical position, as its borders were cocooned by hostility. To the west the Mediterranean Sea seemingly enforces its mass as if binding the Jewish state as Lebanon falls to the north, Syria to the north-east, Jordan to the east, and Egypt lurks to the south-west. Yet, if peace is to prevail, sacrifices have to be made.

Yet many in the surrounding Arab countries feel not enough assurance has been offered by Israel regarding its sincerity to reach a peace settlement, and convinced of it willingness to lay down such sacrifices, as deep down it is felt the children of Israel have suffered enough.

The Mount of Olives is a three-peaked mountain ridge east of Jerusalem; it is so-named because of the olive groves that once covered its slopes. It is said Jesus wept over the plight of Jerusalem as he stood there. On many occasions he would spend time on the mount prophesying to his disciples.

Yosef Salant would wander across the foot of the Mount of Olives towards the garden of Gethsemane at sunrise everyday where he would pray. He would pray for his family, for Jerusalem and its people. He would pray for peace in his land, he would pray that the true Messiah would consume the evil of the Muslim Antichrist and the Christian false prophets on his incarnation bringing about stability and unity within an increasingly divided world.

Yosef would watch the sun slowly rise in the sky; he would watch the spray of light disperse over the ancient tombs across the mount, and he would pray for the dead within them. He would pray for the soul of his brother who had recently been a victim of a suicide bomber that killed many in the city.

Although his Jewish forefathers had been nomadic, this had been the one place on earth that he felt he could never leave; the presence of God was strong, his power and wisdom had been bestowed upon his people in return for their faith and belief. The bond between the children of Israel would continue amidst all the hostility this world could throw at them again and again. Yosef pulled against the wooden staff as he eased himself up from the tree stump where he would sit each morning, his flowing grey beard hung against his ageing face, yet his eyes shone, they shone with the clarity and exuberance of a young man, as the belief in them was strong. He stood for a while watching the daylight slowly spread across the land, yet a darkness shrouded the ground where he stood.

The sun had emerged in the distance, rising across the world as it dispersed the inevitable morning glow. A huge gathering of clouds began to form overhead moving and swirling as one. Yosef's eyes followed the now fulminating mass; as loud cracks of thunder began to bellow from within. It was almost as if the day was somehow reversing, moving backwards towards nightfall.

The wind had built up, moving swiftly through the trees, as the rustle and quiver of each leaf moved across the stillness like whispers; it was as if the souls from the surrounding tombs were eerily calling out to the living.

Speckles of rain began to fall, and he could feel the slight drips across his hands and sandaled feet.

The early morning light had begun to thin; the diminishing sprays of dawn were met by this oncoming dusk. The rain thickened, stirred by a brisk wind. Yosef watched as others began to gather at the foot of the hill. The gathering grew; people began kneeling and praying, some raising their arms openly wailing out loud as they faced the sky above. All he could do was stand and watch as the mild rain now began to fall harder as it developed into a downpour, it fell dripping oozing against the backdrop of where he stood. Yosef held out his hands, all he could do was look upon his outstretched fingers as the rain slithered down his hands like blood from a wound.

He blinked, rubbing his eyes as he could only marvel at the unnatural phenomenon that now presented itself before him. The sky remained dark as what seemed like a billion falling raindrops swirled towards the earth.

Yet as each drop landed, seeping into the world around him, he turned his hands slowly, as tiny droplets landed a deep red, red like blood.

A strange elation fell over him as he recognised the sign of God above. Yosef Salant fell to his knees and began to weep with joy. He had remembered the story his father had told him as a boy, how the tears and sweat of the Messiah had fallen with such grief and anxiety upon the mount, it was fine droplets of blood, and once again his blood would run for the children of Israel.

117

NINETEEN

It had only been recently that she would leave her room, preferring to do so at night when the visitors had long gone home. Sofia Marlow steered the electric wheelchair along the corridor using her "good" right hand to manoeuvre the lever. Her clear blue eyes held no pain or sorrow given her tragic physical state, just a yearning to understand the reasoning for what had happened. The recent operation had proved successful, the "skin substitute" which had provided scaffolding for the multiple grafts needed to rebuild a facial foundation was held together by a plastic mask. The grafts had been taken from the lower back and buttocks, the mask would help to stretch the skin formulating the structure of her new face. The industrial strength sulphuric acid which had been poured into her face had literally melted the skin away, evaporating the skin fats virtually down to the bone. She had emerged a new person, the old Sofia Marlow had gone forever; the injuries down the left arm had withered the skin on the elbow, forearm and fused her fingers together. The process of recovery would be long and hard, with the intervention of psychologists and counsellors to help with the physical and mental challenge that waited. "If I can't have you nobody will." The words had kept echoing inside her head like some far away radio that could not be switched off.

He had seemed so nice, too good to be true, tall and handsome, and in the beginning his "over-attentive nature" was flattering to the point of being overwhelming, and she felt he cared if maybe too much. At first she did not think anything of him meeting her after work, and coincidentally just turning up whenever she was out. It had been the first relationship she had had in two years, and was flattered on how keen he was. His jealousy had pressed upon her with the passing of each day to the point she had found herself making excuses and apologising for him to friends. This had continued to the point she would be bombarded with "probing" questions, her easy-going nature tried to reason with him, but was only met by an intense rage, ignited by the most trivial issue, this had been when he first struck her. She had been spending too much time with certain male colleagues, however innocent this was, and however ridiculous the accusations she was met by something more than unreason, there was a total irrationality to the jealousy revealing this man's insanity. Amidst all the apologies, the "it won't happen again" statements, whatever feeling Sofia had for this man had died. She had decided to end the relationship, and had been surprised how calm he had been. He asked to meet her for one last time, a final drink to say goodbye. He had sounded pitiful, remorseful. Although Sofia had regretted the relationship she had felt a compulsion to end things amicably to tie up a "loose end" in her life and move on.

"I don't blame you," he said clutching her hand tentatively. "It is my fault, I'm an idiot, I know I have a problem," he said pausing. "I guess it is only what I deserve." He continued shaking his head. Sofia had felt a sudden pang of sadness, almost as if those old feelings would resurrect in that moment as he looked into her eyes. But as her thoughts scurried amidst his manipulative nature her resolve returned, Sofia's determination clutched at her common sense, her mind had been made up. The bar had been crowded, and she felt safe, he had been the perfect gentleman apart from the solution he had very discreetly poured into her drink when she had visited the bathroom. Sofia had promised to phone her flatmate and confirm she was still "alive" and he had not turned up with a chainsaw and cut her into little pieces. She walked back towards the crowded bar, yet it seemed to blur in to a haze of garbled noise, then silence, there was a splashing sound inside her head as everything seemed to slow down.

She wobbled on her feet as she unsteadily slumped back into the chair.

Sofia had been sure she had taken only one glass of wine, yet why had she begun slurring her words? Why was she no longer in control?

The next few minutes are fragmented, broken and in disarray in her memory, she remembers been taken outside, the cool air stirring her nostrils, then a sickening feeling as fear crept over her completely as she remembered the car door slamming and being driven away.

She must have been driven for only a few miles when the car slowed down; she had sensed his rage, and it was as if he was miming the vitriolic obscenities he continually yelled towards her.

Sofia had felt a sense of alertness awaken in her mind, yet she was no longer in control of her body, all she could do was lie still at his mercy.

The car had stopped, and then the pain began. At first it was a slight burning sensation across her cheeks and mouth. This uncomforting feeling made her turn her head vigorously from side to side before passing out. Sofia had awoken in the back of the car and felt as if she was floating, there was a constant vibrating feeling across her face as if it had been ripped off, and placed back where it should be but not wholly intact, it felt loose and wet.

She felt movement in her legs as her feet tingled as she slowly began to shuffle off the effects of the drug. He had knelt over her, "Hi baby, it's just you and me, you have got to understand I couldn't let you go, if I can't have you nobody will."

Instinct had begun to shimmer over her, Sofia watched as he began to fill a small glass container from the back of the car and walk back towards her. Whatever he had done to her, she felt she would not survive the outcome; she had to do something and quick. Sofia turned slightly before raising her right leg up towards her chest. He knelt at the edge of the seat, an irrational glee across his face.

She pulled her foot tightly in the stiletto shoe like a fist and waited as he moved closer, for a moment he held the container in a drinking motion before him, teasing her then with every ounce of strength her weary body could summon up she aimed and kicked out.

Sofia rose up on her elbows and began to shuffle towards the edge of the car; his constant screams gave her an exhilarating satisfaction as she could see him clutching his face; he was hurt and she enjoyed his pain.

Although her legs were weak she felt she could move. His screams became more intense shrilling across the wooded area he had taken her. Sofia stood up and walked towards the road that she could just make out in the distance before passing out.

She had been in the hospital for several months and it was only recently the police had interviewed her. Sofia's ex-partner had been arrested at the scene, and he would be blinded permanently from the "acid" wound to his eyes. It had been the first time somebody had used the word "acid".

As usual the hospital was quiet at this time of night; she noticed thin streams of light crept across the floor before her, before pouring out across the corridoor, yet the nightstaff at the end seemed oblivious.

At first she thought there was a fire in the room, as the light seemed so bright, but then she could make out the figure of a man walking forward, clutching the hand of a young boy. Sofia looked upon the face of the man who just smiled at her, she was unable to speak. "Hello Sofia," he said caressing the side of her face, "You shall sleep for a while then you will be reborn onto life." All she could do was cry; she could not understand what stood before her, yet the implications stirred within her being, she wanted to speak, to reach out. What she was witnessing was something she had hoped and prayed for, yet seemed unreal, it could not happen, yet it was, then the light faded and nothing; they were gone as quickly as they came.

The room was vacant and the silence seemed to bite at the air. Sofia turned the wheelchair moving back towards the corridor. She stopped for a moment as she looked at the outline of the mirror from the corner of her eye, Sofia turned to face it, feeling no fear or pain she smiled at her reflection before making her way back towards her room, as she felt the need to sleep.

TWENTY

Nurse Davies smiled as she circled the calendar. May 28th – the well-earned holiday in the sun could not come quick enough. She had slowly scanned the pages of the travel brochure making notes and ticking possible destinations; when her imagination drifted, warm nights and long lingering sandy beaches flickered dreamily across her mind. It seemed a lifetime away as she watched the Christmas lights flicker on and off upon the small tree that had begun to lean annoyingly to one side as it stood at the opening of the central corridor, even the white puffs of falling snow that fell slowly past the windows did not stir any of the season's spirit within her.

She had hated this time of year, this was the reason she would constantly volunteer to do any late shifts during this period.

If she had the choice she would sleep through the "event" awakening when all this unnecessary "crap" was well and truly over with for another year.

Christmas had not been the same since the death of her mother four years earlier. She had watched and tended as multiple sclerosis took its grip, yet all the care and medicine would not prevent the inevitable. In some way Nurse Davies had felt her purpose in life was to prepare these patients for what she felt would be a one-way journey back to non-existence, this had been a bleak perspective pressed upon the everyday working environment she faced, like a gatekeeper between life and death.

She was almost thirty-four years old and had never married; this had been her choice, and she had remained single on her terms. Nurse Davies was not unattractive, quite the opposite, she'd had her admirers. Lately there had been a rumour she had been on several "liaisons" with a senior married doctor, these rumours had a certain malignancy about them and they spread very quickly.

Of course there were the usual promises that he would leave his wife, all she had to do was be patient as he had a lot to lose, she must bear in mind his children, but "most" of all his position. But she would use him as much as she herself was being used, of course she would never tell his wife, she couldn't do with the hassle even though she had hinted on several occasions that she would. Nurse Davies did not see it as blackmail, it wasn't as if he could not afford to give her certain "treats" – she did not like the word payment; he wanted discretion and so did she.

She sighed, glancing at the clock it was only 11:33 p.m. she reached across for the coffee pot, just enough for half a cup before she would start her rounds. Nurse Davies only had to look in on the patients as this time of night most of them would be sound asleep, and it was more for their comfort, and to check all medication had been ingested.

The coffee felt good as she leaned back, her left hand rubbing the back of her neck as she grimaced at the mild aching sensation across her shoulders and at the base of her back she had developed through hours of sitting.

She stood up, turning towards the corridor nearest to the reception area, when something caught her eye. She wasn't sure at first, but it seemed to be a young girl walking towards her.

For the first time Nurse Davies had noticed how quiet it was, and she could not help but feel a certain eeriness stir in and around her confines, as if assuring her of its existence, and she did not know why but she suddenly felt very scared.

She could do nothing but watch as the young girl approached, she was little more than a child, yet there had been something in this child's eyes that Nurse Davies could not avert from.

All the nurse could do was stand still and wait as she approached; how odd a child should be wandering around the hospital late at night, yet her rational thoughts were once again replaced by instinct and fear. Nurse Davies glanced across at the side corridor and felt compelled to run towards it, yet the compulsion held an inward constraint that was beyond her control, a manipulation that forced her to just remain still, and wait.

The girl stood before her smiling, slowly raising her right hand pointing her forefinger towards the nurse.

This child's eyes were not smiling innocent eyes, naïve from the complexities of a grown up world. Instead they were intoxicating and deep, as if too much reason and understanding was held within their perpetual glare, way beyond the years of the girl whose head had now begun to lean curiously to one side.

Nurse Davies felt as if she was looking down upon herself, as the slight shifting sensation trickled through her, her hands and fingers tingled slightly as did the toes on her feet.

She looked across at the window along the opposite side of the corridor; the snow continued to drift past the glass only quicker, swirling amidst the night breeze against the spray of the outside lights.

Her eyes widened at the unusual clarity of vision she now appeared to be in, as she hovered approximately five feet above the ground.

The child began to move her finger and as she did so the nurse moved slowly across mid-air like an apparition. Nurse Davies stopped as she felt the wall opposite the window against her back, and she could feel the smooth concrete against the tips of her fingers. She had wanted to cry out but nothing came, had she fallen asleep and the ghost of her Christmas pasts come to play tricks on her? Come to taunt her, was this in some way her subconscious voice trying to say "Hey! Christmas is not that bad – 'lighten up'– it s not only for the young people, but you can take part as well."?

She had began to shake, yet her body in some way seemed cocooned from her thoughts and inclinations, she was forced to just dangle in mid-air, forced to watch as the girl in front of her began to change.

Nurse Davies could only look upon this mere child as something began to happen, something began to brim from inside. The fear she felt seemed overwhelming as what she hoped was just a strange dream now became a full on surreal nightmare.

At first the girl's fingers had started to stretch, the bones gave a grinding noise as if breaking and reforming inside her hands, and then her skin seemed to ripple across her arms, neck and up through her face. The noise began to throb behind the nurse's eyes, as she turned her head away and began to weep.

The nurse was forced to witness this transformation, as the girl changed, moving and growing into some disproportionate "thing" with an unnatural agility. Bones and sinew continued to stretch as wings now began to form at the back like those of a bat snapping and thrashing against the air like whips.

This creature continued to grow, evolving into something that would only stalk the worst nightmare that could ever exist within the human mind. This demon stood as if it were the true shadow of this seemingly innocent young girl, a true identity against the backdrop of all that seemed good, yet the ultimate personification of evil.

Then as quickly as this hideous image appeared, it was gone, nothing left but the child standing there as before, just watching, smiling resonant; the nurse could only feel the horror still within her, even more so as she continued to look upon the girl who slowly began to clench her fist, still pointing her forefinger at the nurse before quickly swaying her hand towards the window.

Nurse Davies was propelled towards the wooden-framed window section, crashing through with such force that death had been instantaneous; as if for a split second her lifeless body seemed suspended in mid-air before falling limply towards the ground below with the insignificance of a disregarded child's doll.

Abigail Tripp had not found what she was looking for, and a deep anger began to brim from within, trickles of flames began to scurry across the walls around where she stood. A huge fireball was summoned by the mere wave of her hand, roaring across the floors and ceiling.

Windows began to explode as tongues of fire burst through licking against the cold night air. Once again the beast that masqueraded as the child came forth, teeth clenched, slavering, spittle spraying from its huge grotesque mouth as it roared thrashing

125

in an unrelenting rage. This evil that existed from another place that wished to walk upon the world. Wished to reign supreme amidst mayhem, death and destruction, yet it bore a great hunger and it wanted to feed, feed upon the souls of man, upon the sin of man and his temptation.

The beast knew the time was near for the incarnation of the true embodiment of the Messiah, and the beast knew what fate waited if this were to happen.

TWENTY-ONE

Bannerman could not shake of the feeling that had been with him for the past couple of days, something had continually gnawed at him about the recent events. His current problems had been secondary as his focus was redirected towards the strangeness of this case.

The detective stared hard out of the car window, as the outside night seemed to whizz by in a haze. For a while the falling snow stirred memories of his family that he had tried to suppress and keep shut in that rusting trunk deep within his subconscious. In a much "fairer" world he would have been with them, enjoying this perfect seasonal weather with his daughter. Holding his wife tenderly as they watched the little girl sleeping, dreaming her innocent dreams, nothing else mattered in the outside world, robbery, murder; people being beaten to death, small children huddled in doorways with syringes hanging out of their arms. This was something he could expect and handle, everyday events occurring simultaneously by able-bodied human garbage in which he would strive to keep off the streets, and all so the people who led much "fairer" lives could sleep at night.

Instead he was driving across the capital towards the outskirts of Buckinghamshire to some hospital he had never heard of, to see some guy in a wheelchair that would supposedly shed light on these killings, how he was going to do this was something Bannerman could not fathom when prevailing plausibility had been completely overlooked. Yet in light of the other killings in these various countries, a plausible explanation of a serial killer had seemed ludicrous and ruled out, unless there had been several of them working together committing these acts within hours of each other. But why kill priests with such severity? Yet the one thing he was sure of was the timing of these killings, not only was they killed for a reason, rather than random acts by a cult making some deranged statement to the world, yet he felt the time frame of these murders was the common denominator. Whatever the reason, they had to be killed before the coming millennium. Maybe that was the statement in itself. Bannerman had rung through to headquarters and asked for a summary of all information relating to these "global murders", even though he knew the information would be interlinked between other police forces and agencies, and this would take time.

Bannerman did not like where this was going, things just did not "add up"; everything appeared sketchy, like some weird surreal bullshit where religion was the ambivalent cornerstone.

He bit the corner of his lip as his thoughts drifted towards Cardinal Calvi. There had been something about the cardinal that bothered him, amidst the sincerity and his position in the church, there was an underlying motive he sensed within him that just did not seem right. The detectives "knack" had started to kick in, it was a knack that never let him down, as if he could see into the person, see into their lies. "But this was a cardinal for God's sake." The thought made him shake his head slightly, was his paranoia aimed at anything to do with the church?

Did the skin of his paranoia cover his bitterness and resentment towards the church and God himself?

"This resentment will condemn you to hell below, where you will be sent to the paranoid detectives section, where the fires will burn your resentful arsehole for an eternity." Again he shook his head at the absurdity of his thoughts.

"I could do with a drink," he said turning towards Sergeant Foster who was driving.

"After that entire episode earlier Jack, I feel like joining you, that's the strangest shit I have ever seen, in fact it's kind of eerie, if you believe what the cardinal was implying. I didn't catch it all, but these so-called revelations are beyond my understanding, like some kind of conspiracy theory, and to be honest, I don't know what to think," replied Foster, flicking the wipers full on as the snow became more intense.

"Yeah," said Bannerman, "those revelations," he shook his head, "however you look at it, its murder plain and simple. I have hardly touched a drop in the last few days," he continued, examining his unshaved face in the mirror.

"Let's try and keep it that way, Jack, eh?" replied his sergeant. Bannerman acknowledged the concern in his voice nodding in response.

Sergeant Foster was six years older than Jack Bannerman and had moved steadily but slower through the ranks; it was not through lack of ambition, but a steady contentment, he was satisfied with "his lot", he was not interested in the politics of the job, as he knew the responsibility with any given rank, the more prevalent was the politics, and red tape. He was hard working, conscientious and reliable, and had regarded Bannerman more than a superior, he was a friend. Foster had been married to the same girl since he was eighteen, met her on a blind date and the arrow of cupid still protruded firmly from his heart, as it did the first time he laid eyes on her. When Sergeant Foster went home at night he closed his doors on the outside world, locking out the evil of the cesspit he worked in.

He believed in teaching his two sons how important it was to understand the evil that lurks outside of their safe little haven, and to fully understand what people can be capable of doing to each other.

He saw this in some way as an important initiation within their growth into adulthood; he would describe some of the more gruesome cases he had worked on. Foster wanted them to understand the human capabilities to destroy and kill. His message to his children was that life was precious, and it had to be respected, as it would nurture us, the time between a child that grew into a man is moulded by our actions, and choices. He taught them how life could give us anything we wanted, but the easiest thing of all was how quick it could be taken away.

"Do you see anything in the distance Jack?" asked Foster, squinting as he moved towards the windscreen.

"Can't see shit with this snow blowing," replied Bannerman.

"Look – there in the sky," said the sergeant pointing towards the top left of the window.

Flickers of light began moving slowly across the skyline ahead.

"Could be someone's fog lamps," replied Bannerman. Foster turned off the main road, the wheels crunching to an abrupt stop against the fresh snow that had begun to settle. "Wait here," said the detective. As he began to climb out of the car, the coldness and blizzard conditions forced him to cover his eyes.

"There is something in the distance," he continued, pointing towards the flickering light ahead that illuminated the night sky, as it washed down across the treetops.

"That's where the hospital is," said the sergeant pointing. "Something could be wrong Jack; I have a bad feeling about this."

Bannerman got back in the car. "Floor it." Foster quickly responded and the car screeched back onto the road.

They approached the gates of St Michael's and it soon became clear that a section of the hospital was on fire, and it looked serious.

As the car sped along the snow-covered gravel path towards the main entrance, they noticed several people running, patients in wheelchairs being pushed out into the cold night, as it became apparent the fire was now beginning to rage through the north wing of the hospital, spreading swiftly along the corridors towards other sections that ran across the west wing. This was where the children's section was situated within the building.

They stopped the car beside a fire engine; there were another two roaring up the pathway behind them.

Bannerman ran towards the main entrance where he noticed a young nurse coughing hard and weeping against the side of the doorway.

He gripped her arm. "What the hell's happened here?" he asked.

"The fire came out of nowhere," replied the nurse. "It's spreading through the children's section," she continued, weeping. Bannerman knew she was in severe shock and he would not get much sense out of her.

The detective watched as a heavyset black man ran towards him, he was streaked with dirt, carrying a child. He carefully placed the little girl in one of three vacant wheelchairs that had been disregarded by the main reception area, and as he did so the metal braces attached to her thin lifeless legs scraped against the side of the chair as he nearly fell against a water dispenser that had been knocked on its side leaking across the floor.

He gripped one of the ambulance crew to steady himself, who was running back in the direction of the fire amidst several fire officers who were beginning to pull long tubes down the corridor.

"Hey, honey!" said Ethan crouching by the little girl who had begun to whimper softly. "It's okay, I got him. I got Goose." He proceeded to pull out a rather weary looking scraggy monkey in denim dungarees, the cuddly toy had one eye missing, which the child had tried to replace by painting one on its face.

"It's okay Jack, I know this man," said Father Creegan as he gripped Bannerman's arm.

Ethan Cole breathed heavily as he bent over, gripping his knees before rubbing the palms of his hands hard against his eyes, and coughing hard.

"Are you alright Ethan?" asked the priest, placing an arm across his shoulder.

"I got the call about an hour or so ago," he replied. "I had not long left, and I got back here as quick as I could." Ethan shook his head as the words stumbled from his mouth before standing upright. "Man, I just can't believe it," he continued, "this damn fire spread so quickly as if it had a mind of its own."

"Where is Gabriel Salmach?" demanded Cardinal Calvi as he appeared in the doorway followed by his two bodyguards.

Ethan just held out his hands before replying, "That's what I don't understand," he continued wide-eyed, "I don't know, and Ben Mills, his... his room was empty."

This stark realisation seemed to prompt the physiotherapist, "But Ben was already dead, well almost anyway." He said this more to himself than those that stood around him, as if he was trying to make sense of what was going on. "Most of the patients had been moved in time to the rear section of the hospital, as the fire was moving along the opposite direction, the rest of the patients that could move by themselves in their wheelchairs, came through here, or were brought down out front. But Ben and Gabriel... man I just don't know," he said incredulously. "They sure ain't in any shape to just get up and walk out of here," he continued, shaking his head again.

Bannerman frowned, looking over at Sergeant Foster who was putting his coat around the sobbing nurse. The sergeant acknowledged Bannerman's puzzled look as they both looked upon Ethan with a bemused curiosity.

"We gotta find them," said Ethan, anger stirring in his tone, as he was both overcome by panic and exhaustion. "This goddamn fire, why here? Of all places a hospital." Bannerman watched as a large dark car approached, and just parked in the distance. The engine fell silent and for a moment there was no movement, until the driver's door slowly opened.

Bannerman cupped his hands as he walked across towards the vehicle; he watched as the driver rushed around towards the rear passenger door and quickly opened it.

The passenger emerged, and for a moment just observed the burning section of the hospital. Bannerman could not help but notice how tall he was, had to be 6'3"-6'4" thought the detective as the man approached him. "I am Detective Inspector Bannerman." The man wore the same distinctive black galero as Cardinal Calvi; he had an air of importance dressed in a red trimmed black cassock, as he stood before the detective. "I am Monsignor Gerard P Raffin, from the Vatican," he announced. "Forgive me... sir," said Bannerman, "but one of your... colleagues is already here, a Cardinal Calvi."

"This fire has been started deliberately," said the Monsignor. "Get as many people away from here, as quickly as possible, he has been here." There was calmness in his voice as he studied the detective.

Bannerman walked over towards him. "We are not getting much sense out of anyone tonight; could you elaborate to whom you are referring to? Who has been here?" Monsignor Raffin could detect anger in the detective's voice.

At first the Monsignor did not reply as he walked around Bannerman continuing to survey the fire, "There are many titles to his identity," he said, placing his arms behind his back, his voice resolute, "Diablo, Lucifer, Belial but you will know him simply as the Devil."

Bannerman shook his head but remained silent. "I can detect by your silence, that you do not believe me Inspector Bannerman," said the Monsignor turning to face him. Bannerman watched as he signalled towards the car, two men emerged from the vehicle, dressed in black cassocks rushing across towards the entrance. "This evil knows no bounds," he continued. "It is little wonder this hospital has not been completely destroyed and raised to the ground, he is looking for something, Detective, and as yet... he has not found it."

"Look!" he replied. "All I know is we were coming to this hospital to speak to somebody who could help in two separate murder inquiries that so happen to be priests." This guy is just stirring this whole pile of shit with a different paddle, thought Bannerman.

Two more dark cars appeared parking just in front of where they both were stood. "As I said before, one of your colleagues is here, a car...."

"Inspector!" interrupted the Monsignor, "Cardinal Emilio Calvi was found murdered a little over a week ago, I hope this in some way illustrates the gravity of this situation."

"So we have somebody impersonating one of your people?" asked the detective.

"You could say that," replied the Monsignor as he handed Bannerman a photograph, before walking off towards the hospital. For a few moments the detective stared at the picture of the man who he had been talking to less than a few hours earlier, and something other than the weather conditions had caused his hands to shake.

TWENTY-TWO

The chanting grew louder as the young naked girl was carried across towards the black covered main high altar. The hooded figures carefully placed her upon the top, and she did not scream or cry out.

Fine trickles of blood had begun to run down each side of her face, as the raw pentacle-like symbol that looked like it had been torn across her forehead was still fresh.

The audience stood ceremoniously, a mixture of the "social elite", rich businessmen in oil and aerospace industries. MPs and judges rubbed shoulders with solicitors, doctors and various members of the House of Lords. Many of these *societates clandestinae* or secret societies had been gathering anxiously throughout the last few days within the diminishing hours of the century.

Large black candles flickered around the altar as this elite mass gathered transfixed in an almost hypnotic state. Yet their eagerness and anticipation portrayed an almost animal-like guise as they awaited the kill, chanting in the same eerie unison.

There had been many "organisations" spread throughout the country and across the world. Satanists had been regarded as pre-Christian, coming from the pagan image of power, sexuality, sensuality and virility. Whereas Satan can be seen as a force of nature, and of course a form of travesty of Christian ritual. Yet there are those who believe that Satan "a banished angel from heaven" has nothing to do with hell or evil.

But worshippers of the Devil see him as the highest force, and worship him as a god. Devil worshippers hold their ceremonies with the purpose to gain power from the Devil himself. This worship is seen as the first stage in the evolution of religion, as we will always fear the bad not the good.

The Grand Master stood by the altar, candles burned slowly, as trails of smoke drifted up through the air forming a vaporous canopy overhead. His figure shimmered in the faint light.

The blade seemed to flash across the darkness menacingly as he spread his arms out wide. His left hand bore two disfigured fingers that had been fused together, the aftermath of a fire. The crowd began to gather closer as their chanting grew louder. They stood against the forefront of what could only be described as an opening, some kind of gateway hanging transparent against the periphery of a great depth within.

What seemed like constant winds blowing and curling against the distance within this "gateway" became more apparent as the chanting abruptly ceased. There was something else, something other than winds howling; it was screams and pleading, terror-filled voices distant and far away, building up within the constraints of the earth, and it seemed to be moving closer.

The Grand Master's hands joined as one as he held the large knife above the girl who still looked blankly ahead, her mind induced by an unnatural grip compelling her body to obey the oncoming inception towards her inevitable oblivion.

"Oh master I offer thee the soul of this being." There was no hesitation as he plunged the knife swiftly into the girl who could only groan faintly, as life oozed out of her. The unnatural constriction within her being instilled a silence. And for a moment, her trance-like state opened up the realisation that was to be her fate as a tear fell down the side of her face.

There was a sound of glee and urgency from the crowd, and their anticipation grew stronger, their expectancy heightened as the cries and screams from the "gateway" became louder. The crowd stood like expectant children not fully understanding the depth of this terror that would unleash itself upon the world through their simple naivety, and inner search for a higher excitement within their pathetic lives. This zest and yielding for some unearthly manifestation to bear forth would as they wish, reveal an inherent evil in absolute bodily form, to befall their expectant glare.

They watched as the young girl walked by and stood by the throne-like chair at the side of the Grand Master. A smile gathered at the corners of the child's mouth, then she began to change, the crowd stood back gasping. Her small body erupted into multiple deformities.

The crowd fell to their knees in a sort of terror-unified worship, before the Grand Master walked forward, inviting them to rise. Though at first hesitant, everyone rose accordingly, yet edging backwards as this manifestation began to grow. They watched as the bones and sinew stretched, breaking and reforming as the creature took shape. There was a sudden urgency from the screams and cries that continued to pour forth from the "gateway" as if in some way offering an appeasement that would influence the outcome of their eternal suffering and damnation.

The demon began to rise up upon the dais, and the assembled dignitaries looked upon their chosen lord and master in fervent anticipation, as they continued to chant.

The creature's wings spread out from its back, then continued to thrash back and forth, as it stood before its flock in its grotesque entirety, slavering and snarling as its huge head scanned the gathering, savouring their fear and absolute obedience.

The Grand Master raised his hands, as innumerable hosts had begun to pour forth up through the eternal domain, up through the gateway, lingering at the forefront of the beast.

"The time is almost upon us," said the Grand Master. "We must go forth within these diminishing hours in search of the Christ and destroy him; he must be destroyed within his embodiment of flesh and blood."

A feverish chanting began to fill the air, as the crowd, of whom some were high-ranking police offers, as were many other well-heeled dignitaries that were placed within powerful positions within mainstream society, slowly began to disperse.

This vast connected web scoured the many corridors of power, spreading across the world relentless in their goal as the new millennium approached.

TWENTY-THREE

Detective Bannerman stood by the hospital entrance just clutching the photo the Monsignor had handed to him. "He's gone," said Foster, "even the bodyguards, vanished!"

"Sorry!" replied Bannerman, just looking through his sergeant, as his mind lay elsewhere.

"Cardinal Calvi..." continued the sergeant raising his eyes, "the closest I have seen to thin air, as soon as the Monsignor turned up, he was gone, what's going on Jack?" he asked shaking his head. "The guy on this photo, I was talking to earlier at the crime scene in the church, was murdered approximately a week ago," replied Bannerman handing the picture to his sergeant.

One of the men in black cassocks whispered something in the Monsignor's ear before handing what looked like a videotape discreetly to him.

Bannerman approached the two men.

"I will take that Monsignor; this is police business and my jurisdiction, that tape could hold some 'rational' answers to what actually caused this."

Monsignor Raffin's companion or evident bodyguard, stood in front of Bannerman menacingly, the detective could not help noticing this "man of God" had an air of danger around him as he frowned at the detective; he was young, early thirties, and in some way the simple black cassock only extenuated the bulk of his frame, he had the build and appearance of a navy seal, his clear blue eyes studied the detective with a cold determination in them that threw out a warning like he was some kind of religious mercenary. "Looks like the Vatican had their own ideas on security personal," thought the detective. "If you don't want this man arrested, I suggest you let me do my job, Monsignor." Bannerman glared across at Monsignor Raffin who nodded towards his companion.

"This tape must be studied immediately," said the Monsignor, as he handed it to the detective.

"Hey! There is a VCR machine across the way in the office by reception," said Ethan, as he pointed towards the corner side doorway.

Bannerman squinted as he fast-forwarded the videotape. They watched, as the screen became a slow blur as it flickered against the backdrop of the office.

"Hey, slow down," said Ethan, his forefinger almost touching the glass as he anxiously moved forward.

"Right there," he continued, "that kid, I have seen that little girl before."

Bannerman had begun to rewind the tape before clicking the play button. They watched as the video ran, flicking between different areas of the hospital as the usual array of doctors and nurses went about their designated duties, porters taking patients to various locations around the hospital wards, nothing seemed out of the ordinary.

"Move the time frame forward, that's earlier in the day, and you have rewound too far." The detective frowned at Ethan. When he clicked the play button the timer displayed at the top right hand corner of the screen.

"This is now within the last couple of hours," said Monsignor Raffin.

"Yeah and there she is again," replied Ethan.

"What the hell is it with this child?" interrupted Bannerman. "Surely it's got to be a patient or member of the family, they do get visitors here don't they?"

"Yeah sure, but look at the time, when she first appears it's 11.09, all visitors have left by 9.30, and most of the patients have severe back and leg trauma, in other words, walking is the last thing they can do."

Ethan sat back in the swivel chair turning towards the others, "I... I thought I had seen this child earlier, as I left the hospital after I finished my shift."

For a moment he paused, looking across at the detective.

"Please continue," said Monsignor Raffin.

"Well it was outside in the parking lot," he went on. "The snow had begun to fall, I was heading towards my car, and I thought, well no, I was sure she was stood at the far side of the lot, this small figure out alone in the dead of night just watching me." Again Ethan paused, "I went over, but there was nothing, well almost nothing."

"What do you mean?" asked Father Creegan walking around towards the rear of the room.

"Her footprints!" replied Ethan, "Two small fresh imprints in the gathering snow, right there where she was stood," he shook his head. "Look! I know what I saw, and then she just vanished! Something weird is going on," he went on, again shaking his head.

"I think we need to get all the security tapes in the hospital back to the station," said Bannerman standing up.

"Look!" yelled Ethan, his finger pressed against the screen, "It's her."

"He's right," said Foster edging towards the physiotherapist, "She is just standing there, a young girl."

They watched in silence as the girl just stood at the end of a corridor, before slowly walking down towards a nurse who was sat at a desk along the crossway of the four adjoining corridors that met at the far end.

A silence gathered in the small office apart from a faint whirring of the tape machine. The nurse began to stand as she acknowledged the child approaching her. All they could do was look upon the screen within the stirring silence and bear witness to what could only be described as "extreme surreal events" unfolded before them.

"Holy shhh…" Ethan covered his mouth almost falling back over the chair, as he quickly began to stand.

"Silence!" demanded the Monsignor, as he moved towards the screen.

The girl slowly pointed her forefinger towards the nurse in a command-like gesture, and then as she moved her hand. The nurse began to rise in mid-air, as her lingering body was placed against a wall at the far side of the desk, following in unison, against the girl's movements.

"Good Lord!" said Father Creegan, as they watched this seemingly innocent child begin to change, deforming into something hideous. What stood before them was not of this world, a grotesque creature detailed in its entirety almost like some great illusion against the forefront of reality, which was questionable against the stability of sane belief.

"Jesus Christ, what the hell is that?" said Foster, this time not apologising for his contrary outburst in front of these religious dignitaries.

Bannerman just stared ahead at the screen in silence not knowing what to say or do as he was caught up in the events before him. The creature continued to change in horrific proportions, large wings burst out of its back, snapping against the air. But what they were witnessing, although completely surreal looked as if it had been some kind of illusion, as it was gone, nothing but the girl again. The creature had gone, had it been something they had imagined?

The monitor began to crackle as interference distorted the picture, but not before the nurse who continued to just linger at the mercy of this "beast" or thing, was seemingly hurled across the air crashing through the window at the opposite side, her body broken as it fell limply below.

Father Creegan covered his eyes, turning away from the screen. The Monsignor stood in silence bowing his head and made the sign of the cross. Bannerman continued to watch as if any reaction was still subdued by his scepticism. He stared hard at the screen, it was as if the young girl was staring back at them, she smiled raising her hand, as if aware of her audience. For a moment the detective found it hard to avert from her stare, flames had begun to rise around her, licking at the air as they spread.

The screen continued to crackle with the white noise interference, as they noticed the fire that had started a couple of hours ago. This fire they had witnessed on the tape was now actually occurring within the video monitor.

Small flames began to creep from the video slot. "Get the tape," shouted the Monsignor, as the flames began to grow and spread around the monitor moving across the small table it was rested on.

Jack Bannerman remained unusually quiet, continuing to just stare blankly as if he was in another place, not fully acknowledging what was happening. The Monsignor's young bodyguard tried to eject the video, but was hurled against the wall as the glass from the screen sprayed outwards, as the monitor exploded. He fell hard against the floor, yelling as fine shards of glass embedded across his face and forehead. Bannerman gripped him by the forearm attempting to pull him up, "not so tough now eh?" thought the detective before he himself was forced to shield his eyes as the glass from one of the office windows was suddenly blown into the room, hurling the detective backwards, and reeling over a stack of post trays.

They watched as the fire continued to spread, running down the legs of the table, moving outwards across the floor in all directions. It was as if the fire had reason and purpose, as it now began to circle them, moving across the ceiling.

Ethan pulled a fire extinguisher from beside the doorway; he quickly snapped the seal, spraying the foam across the floor and against the burning monitor. Sergeant Foster tried to pull open the door which appeared "stuck". A fine line of flames quickly rushed up and around the inner frame, before creeping up towards the ceiling gathering and joining as one mass of fire.

Two of the Monsignor's "cardinals" began to kick at the outer door which was now completely ablaze.

The flames continued to move around the small office, as the extinguisher had little effect. The younger cardinal staggered to his feet, pushing Sergeant Foster out of the way. He quickly pulled a small hand pistol from inside his cassock and carefully aimed at the door lock before firing off several rounds. He began kicking at the door, and even though the lock was shot out, the door remained firmly "wedged shut".

A second pane of glass was blown inwards again sending the bodyguard hurling across the room. Sergeant Foster rushed towards him, he noticed small glass splinters covered his face but blood started to pour freely down his cheek and neck, as a larger piece had embedded itself below his left eye.

Bannerman rushed at the still defiant door with his shoulder, the force was enough to almost split it across the middle, the impact sending him reeling to his knees. Ethan and the sergeant continued to kick what remained of the door out into the corridor.

One by one they quickly made their way out of the small office as the now roaring fire began spewing out of the doorway like huge grasping hands. Father Creegan was the last to leave, yet the fire seemed to cover the entrance as if anticipating his only choice of escape, beckoning him. Ethan jumped back through, "Let's go," said the physiotherapist gripping him by the shoulder, "Cover your eyes Father," he continued almost dragging the priest through the burning doorway.

They watched as the fire began to recede across the room, diminishing, as if being pulled back along the walls, into a reluctant defeat, summoned back to its origins, like the last remnants of a genie being drawn towards its lamp.

Monsignor Raffin walked across towards Jack Bannerman.

"These last remaining days and hours will prove to be the most important in all of human history; you have witnessed a fragment of what this evil is capable of." He paused for a moment, turning, averting his attention across towards the mayhem within the hospital's vicinity. "The hell we are all aware of." He raised his eyes, nodding, as he faced the detective, "That same hell that some of us dare even doubt that exists," Bannerman could detect an inner strength that seemed to permeate, within and around this man, yet it seemed to bind itself within a tight constraint of fear that could not be hidden. "Shall turn itself inside out upon your own cynical world, Detective, unleashing an evil totally unprecedented against anything we could ever do to each other, or have ever done within our history, it is imperative we find the Christ, while he still remains flesh and blood." The Monsignor's eyes narrowed towards Bannerman, "Our very existence depends on it."

TWENTY-FOUR

The snow had fallen hard that day, as it had fallen harshly for the past three days, illuminating the land amidst the gloom of the winter months that seemed to crawl upon each coming hour. Nebi gazed out upon the hills and naked trees, whose white spine-like branches dipped and curved like cracks against the vast expanse of nothingness that surrounded their home. He gazed through the window at the thick falling snow as in a slow uniform continuity it descended upon the stillness of the land.

Disillusioned was probably the wrong way to describe how he felt; yes he had been confused and he had every right to be.

He had continued to follow Maxim Wessler for several weeks, monitoring his whereabouts reporting back to the British government.

It would soon become obvious that this man's agenda followed a very different route, as did the many town hall officials and various members of the police force itself. And Nebi would soon come to realise that this web had been spreading outward for some time.

Wessler was a Nazi, the ultimate evil that had been thrust upon mankind in recent times. An immorally degenerate organisation whose fundamental goals had been control of the economy, racist nationalism and national expansion, which in a fervent culpability led to mass genocide, thus willingly carried out by its equally degenerate members.

But this was no underlying motive to resurrect this organisation as thought, no phoenix bearing swastikas rising from the burning allied flames that eventually destroyed it. Nebi had discovered the underlying direction of worship was directed elsewhere.

This need to worship had become an undercurrent of fervent activity that surged without hesitation amongst the "higher classes" of society, like an indiscriminating disease it had now begun to spread across mainstream society, devouring any inward reservations to what was deemed right.

Nebi had followed Wessler to the outskirts of the frontier borders towards the hill country.

He had always appeared to be heavily guarded and deeply revered by those around him; it was almost as if he himself was being worshipped. Nebi had been careful to stay out of site as he followed the procession of cars that came to a stop within the grounds of what could only be described as a large opaque building jutting against the skyline like an elaborate citadel. Yet it stood without lustre as if a fulminating gloom weaved around its exterior.

He had watched through binoculars at the gathering crowd stood in silence unified in dark flowing robes, a soft chanting spreading as they began to walk towards the entrance.

He had to get closer to the building. Nebi began to make his way around a small acute ridge narrowing outwards across the rock face he stood upon. He watched as two men stood outside the main entrance, while two more patrolled along the side at each end.

Nebi had to be swift as he quickly moved along the ridge as he would be in full view, yet he was shielded partially from the weather conditions, he continued to make his way towards the rear of the building.

He had been on "surveillance missions" before, yet never had his anticipation and awareness been pushed to such a heightened level; he felt fearful of the outcome whatever it may be.

He scaled down along a narrow passageway that ran three-quarters across the rear. A large steel doorway that looked like it had not been opened in years blocked the opening, cutting the passageway short. For a while he just waited, the chanting he heard earlier filtered out through the walls.

Many of the windows had been blocked up, and those that were not had bars running down them. He walked along the remaining passageway which seemed to darken towards the end. There was a cast-iron pipe that ran from the edge of the roof down towards a drainage grid where he stood. Nebi began to climb towards a small ledge underneath a window. Gripping the rim of the pipe, resting his left foot upon the ledge, he knelt down peering through the fine film of grime covering the small window. For a moment he half expected Adolf Hitler himself addressing the audience with a blazing rhetoric flurry of emotions. Instead he could see the large gathering of hooded figures congregating around what looked like a small altar, he watched as they slowly lowered their hoods. Many of the people in the gathering appeared to be from different nationalities around the world, yet all with one common aim in their pursuit and search for some kind of inner sanctum within this house of evil.

The chanting continued to filter through the walls only to be swallowed up by the wind that began to curl and rasp against the sides of the passageway. Nebi gripped one of the bars swinging his legs against a small ledge on the opposite side where a window or opening once stood that had long been bricked up. He slowly gained more leverage pulling him-self up, resting his arms against the edge of the window ledge; he ran his hand against the frosted glass.

He noticed Wessler, and many of the people of Villach, yet as he peered into the dull exterior he also noticed many of those he had corresponded with in the previous weeks.

These were people who he shared information with and had trusted, people whom he had regarded as colleagues who like himself worked for the British government. He shook his head at the confusion he felt swirling before him.

Nebi watched as Wessler addressed the crowd who looked on trance-like, yet there was an eerie glee of anticipation within their manner that he found unnerving.

He knew this was something more than the re-emergence of Nazism, this was something more sinister.

Maxim Wessler raised his arms out wide and the crowd began to back away bowing down. Two hooded men dragged a man towards the altar from a side room. They approached Wessler, throwing the man to the ground before him. Wessler in turn gripped him turning the man around to face the crowd, who once again began to chant. Nebi rubbed his hand against the frosted glass peering closer. He had recognised the man; he was the priest from St Jacob's.

He watched as if in slow motion Maxim Wessler pulled what looked like a ceremonial dagger from inside his robe. Nebi felt his heart pumping faster in his chest, his eyes widened as he almost yelled out as he witnessed Wessler without hesitation slowly slit the man's throat; he stood holding him before the crowd like a trophy, while the blood from his wound sprayed out across the floor.

Nebi could only watch as the dying man sank to his knees clutching the wound, blood seeped through his fingers rolling down the back of his hands, his eyes open, and soft intermittent gurgling sounds emitting from his mouth as he fell forward.

Nebi dropped down from the window crouching in the passageway amidst the silence; he felt alone, and an impending fear befell him. He had just witnessed a senseless murder of a man of God, in turn witnessed by what he had regarded as colleagues, and agents he had worked with in the "field", people he had to trust, and they seemed to be part of whatever was going on, standing there as if mesmerised like schoolchildren relishing a simple playground fight.

For a moment he was snatched from his confused thoughts, turning peering towards the end of the passageway, as something was moving towards it.

He quickly got to his feet backing up against the wall, carefully moving towards the edge of the opening.

The continued crunching of snow told him it had to be one of the guards approaching. Nebi crouched down anticipating the guard turning in towards the passageway.

For a moment the footsteps stopped. Nebi's breathing was very slight, his heart still thundered in his chest so loud the Italian border patrols could have located him. He waited, listening carefully against the entrance; he thought he could hear what he thought was a match being lit.

Slowly the guard walked across towards the centre of the opening before stopping abruptly. He moved the cigarette from his mouth and just stared across the passageway floor.

Nebi forced himself against the side of the archway obscuring himself from the guard, who was now staring down intently at the fresh footprints in the snow.

He knew this man had to act distinctively on two things, his professionalism or his inquisitiveness. If he were a pro he would quickly radio through, yet he knew the guard's inquisitiveness would get the better of him. As the guard began to walk through the passageway Nebi struck him on the side of the head hard, then swinging around with the ridge of his hand he caught him full in the throat with enough force to send him crashing against the opposite wall to the entrance, before throwing a clean punch connecting with the man's jaw knocking him unconscious.

He quickly gripped the guard's ankles, pulling him along the passageway floor towards the steel door where he placed his body across the bottom of the doorway like a human draft excluder.

Nebi knew it was only a matter of time before they noticed the guard was missing but hopefully enough time for him to get away.

The one thing that was on his side was the weather, as the snow fell blowing into a blizzard, it would not be long before the guard's body would be covered by the elements before he woke up or was discovered.

He ran to the end of the passageway carefully glancing along either side of the opening before running across towards the edge of the woodlands that covered the bottom of the foothills, the continued chanting still stirred in his ears.

Nebi had a strong urge to get to his family; he could sense evil within the building, an unnatural evil. The compulsion was strong to get away from this place to get within the safe sanctuary of his home. He continued to look around, expecting a mass of hooded figures following him. Unbeknown to Nebi his movements were being watched long before he had scaled along the ridge and down the rock face and entered the passageway.

TWENTY-FIVE

Gabriel Salmach had remembered his mother wrapping the collars of his coat around his neck, tucking the knot of the red scarf into his jumper; she kissed him on the forehead, playing with his fringe. The snow had painted the land a "crystal sheet" white. "Say goodbye Gabriel," said his mother as she clutched his hand waving towards their house that had been their home for the past two years.

The boy had remembered a feeling of reluctance that tingled throughout his body; there was an inner feeling of dread that his young years shielded from his understanding. Nebi had tried to explain to his wife the reason for their swift departure, the sudden need to leave what he could only describe as imminent danger around them. He could not be specific at what he had witnessed, as he did not fully understand it himself, but he knew that it was spreading very quickly and not just here but everywhere. He had also felt like a rabbit caught in a maze within the fox's den. He had almost wished it had been something as simple as an underground resurrection of Nazism.

They were to meet a contact at a checkpoint along the Italian borderline who would issue them with flight tickets back to England.

The car weaved along the Tyrolean landscape, as they marvelled at the dense coniferous forests that stretched along the lower slopes of the alpine province. Nebi had thought about the brief conversation on the phone with Jonathan Frazier, how the indifference in his voice stirred with a coldness as he had tried to explain what he had seen, and who he had seen witnessing it. Jonathan Frazier had taken over the helm of the organisation after the horrific murder of his father, Sir Reginald, who had been found mutilated within the grounds of his home.

The small Fiat the family had travelled in had been followed unnoticed for some time by a black Mercedes-Benz 300sel saloon. The car sped up, weaving along the narrow mountain road towards the smaller vehicle.

Nebi had noticed the oncoming car heading towards them in the rear-view mirror, approaching fast. He moved towards the side of the road to let the Mercedes pass, but it just sped up, slowing as it approached directly behind them. Nebi wound the window down sticking his left hand out in a signal gesture to wave the car on, but it continued to sit behind them menacingly.

"Why is he driving like that?" asked Olivia, her fingers began to tremble. Nebi sensed the agitation in her voice as she hugged Gabriel tightly against her.

"He is probably lost," he replied, looking into the rear-view mirror only to be met by Gabriel's round eyes, as he looked intently at his father as if he was sharing the same concern he was hiding from his wife.

The Mercedes moved closer, touching the rear bumper. Olivia screamed out; Nebi put his foot down tying to edge away but the Mercedes just sped up, shunting the smaller car full on. He tried to control the vehicle, but it hit the guardrails catching the rear end as he managed to steer across towards the opposite side of the road. The pursuing car relentlessly followed.

Olivia began to scream hysterically, the narrow mountain road opened up and Nebi knew he could not outrun such a powerful car. He began to turn the Fiat erratically from side to side with a mixture of both anger and desperation. He could see in the distance what seemed like a downturn in the road's gradual erosion, causing the guardrails to curve outwards. Although the road was wider, the slope on either side was greater as it dipped precariously towards the tumbling dense forests below.

The Mercedes crashed against the car relentlessly, buffeting it, before moving alongside. Nebi stared hard at the blacked out windows as it crashed against his driver's door, forcing it to swerve dangerously close to the edge. He had managed to keep control until it was hit again.

For a moment, time seemed to slow down as the Fiat was forced over the side down towards the ravine, hurling through the air, spinning, landing crushing the underside of the roof as it toppled against the side of a tree, before breaking into several pieces like shattering glass in the slow deliberate aftermath.

Gabriel had been flung from the car, his fall had been broken by dense foliage but the child had landed badly.

Nebi reached across towards his wife who was bleeding seriously from a head wound, there was blood trickling from her ear, as she lay unconscious. He tried to move her, calling out her name, but his own movements were restricted as the impact had forced the front of the car inwards as the steering wheel had embedded him against his seat.

His thoughts remained muddled, as he tried to focus, blurred abstractions shimmered around him, he could smell burning, he quickly forced some of the broken windscreen out across the car bonnet, this was when he noticed a figure standing at the top of the ravine.

Although blurred the outline of the figure remained still, just watching them, until his eyes focussed upon the familiarity of the man... It was Phillip Rackman.

The sudden realisation of the passing seconds seemed to hang before him like an eternity. He looked up at Rackman's seemingly bloodless expression, standing at the top of the ravine; his hands were folded, yet he clutched something. Nebi looked upon the long smooth barrel; he could see it was a weapon.

Nebi knew he was at the mercy of forces he did not understand. He had been the perpetrator many times, but as the sun set upon his sudden clarity, he had realised like a pawn constantly pushed around the chess board, he had been ordered to orchestrate the inevitable outcome of many, and many of those he had been sent to kill were opposed to the evil that was now about to kill him. *He had killed men of God.* These men had been sent to infiltrate this evil, sent by the church, and as soon as their identities were revealed, sometimes by their own "inner sanctum", as this evil walked along many corridors of power, in many guises.

He had been used, and now his sudden curiosity had begun to outweigh his usefulness. His faith had remained strong, even though the penance would be his life. He had felt some inner assurance that his existence upon the earth would not end with his death, his legacy would transcend his predicament and he felt ready. Nebi Salmach sat back in the seat looking up at Phillip Rackman who was aiming the gun towards the fuel tank.

Gabriel had been aware of what was to take place, it had been foreseen, and he knew he would survive. It would be almost two days before the child was found barely alive. He was taken to the nearest hospital across the Italian border. The doctor who had first examined the child could not help notice an unusual calmness about the boy, it was as if the injuries were secondary, like he relinquished any feeling of pain, and just cocooned himself within some sort of bubble of serene tranquillity.

Gabriel Salmach would awake in the following days to a world without his parents, and a world he could no longer walk upon, as he would be paralysed from the waist down for the rest of his life. He would have to endure both physical and mental trauma, he would need to reach within his human capabilities for that inner strength that can sometimes abandon us. Gabriel would have to find his faith and belief by his own understanding.

TWENTY-SIX

It had always felt like a headmaster's office, that stark offi-cious odour hung in the air like some annoying hierarchy stench, permeating the overhanging authority it was meant to.

Bannerman sat in the small leather-bound chair, which creaked as he continually moved and fidgeted trying to find comfort in something that was an appropriate fixture, designed more for its aesthetic presence than for just sitting on.

Photographs and certificates adorned the walls around the room, all accomplishments of his superior, who as the pictures and years within them fluctuated, so did the ever-displaying overdone regimented poses at various stages of his career.

"A bit too much self-assurance at one's own achievements," thought Bannerman, as he studied the wall behind the oak-veneered desk. At the side was a large bookcase stacked with an impressive collection of military literature, varying battles in the Second World War, also accompanied by distinguished British and German generals, in a row of neatly leather-bound volumes, all standing side by side in chronological order.

Chief Superintendent Blake did not look up at first; instead choosing to remain within the self-appointed silence a little longer than necessary, this was something all people in authority seemed to do, and had always inwardly annoyed Jack Banner-man. He was not sure if it was ignorance, or some intimidation tactic, a kind of gentle reminder of "Hey! I'm the guy in charge around here let's not forget that eh?" The scribbling across his report broke the uneasy silence, his manner and demeanour went hand in hand with his stoic nature.

"How have you been Jack?" asked the superintendent, his eyes moving across the document he was studying, slowly glancing above the thin-rimmed glasses towards the detective.

"Bearing up well under the circumstances thank you sir," replied Bannerman.

"Yes Jack," said Blake, removing his glasses, studying the detective. "How is your wife?" The superintendent sat back in his far more comfortable swivel chair. Bannerman leaned forward feeling discomfort in the question.

"Not good, sir, only time will tell, the death of our..." He paused clearing his throat, yet could not bring himself to say the word daughter, "Of Ashley, hit her very hard. The doctors say she refuses to accept it, and has retreated within herself, closing herself down to the reality of what has happened; only she can come out of it."

"I am sorry Jack, you have my sympathy."

"Thank you, sir."

The superintendent clasped his hands together tightly again, studying the detective. Bannerman felt the intensity in his boss's eyes like a spider watching a tangled fly before it pounced.

"Have we any updates on this business with the priests?" For a moment Bannerman shook his head delaying the reply.

"Well to be honest, sir, I have witnessed many murders in my time, but this... the ferocity," his words stumbling from his mouth, as he held up his hands questionably, "What I am trying to say," he continued, "without stating the obvious religious connotations, I am searching for some logic within what has become a mixture of circumstantial illogic. There is plenty in this case that goes beyond my understanding, occurrences that infer something that falls within the realms of fiction."

Bannerman paused, before continuing, "Eleven priests from different locations around the world all seemingly killed within hours of each other." Again the detective shook his head.

"Yes Jack it is baffling me too, but we better come up with answers and soon, as some serious heavyweights from the Vatican are crawling all over the department." Blake rose to his feet, "I have to report direct to the Deputy Prime Minister. Various intelligence agencies from across the world are starting to breathe down our necks, and I don't have to mention the ramifications stirred by every religious puritanical fruitcake crawling out of the woodwork when the papers get fully hold of it."

"Of course not, sir," replied Bannerman. "Do we know why the words ANNO DOMINI were left on the bodies?" asked the superintendent once more scrutinising the detective's reply.

Bannerman held out his hands, shaking his head. "Again, sir, the words mean in a specified year of the Christian era, in the year of our Lord, a thousand year cycle; it seems leaving them on the bodies was not only meant as some kind of message, but essentially a denunciation of Christianity."

"I am aware of their meaning," said Blake.

"It had all the hallmarks of some kind of deranged killers maybe working in unison, at least that was my thinking," replied Bannerman.

Superintendent Blake moved forward. "What do you mean?" he asked, his eyes narrowing curiously.

"Look, sir, it's… well it's bizarre, that's the only way I can describe the recent events I have witnessed."

"Please continue," said Blake, sitting at the edge of his desk. "The fire at St Michael's, we know was no accident, and there was something on the video tape that was well," Bannerman raised his eyes before continuing, "was horrific, a young girl changing, deforming into some kind of monster, a creature not of this world." For a few moments there was a silence between the two men.

"I am aware how it sounds, sir, it sounds like something out of a third-rate horror flick. At first I thought it was a trick, some kind of special effect, an illusion, but we had all seen it, then the monitor and screen just burst into the flames, as if it had a mind of its own."

"It seems this nonsense is spreading," said Blake, picking up a newspaper at the side of the desk, handing it to Bannerman. RAIN FALLS THE COLOUR OF BLOOD IN THE HOLY CITY read the headlines across the front page.

"What do you know of Gabriel Salmach?" asked Blake.

"Well, not a great deal," he replied. "He was a patient at the hospital, dead or alive, we are not sure, nothing was found, most of the other patients were moved in time, there were just two unaccounted for, Salmach and the whereabouts of a young boy, Ben Mills. What we don't understand," continued Bannerman, "Gabriel is paraplegic and the boy was clinically dead, but they were both gone, nothing, no trace, no remains nothing, like I said bizarre."

"It gets weirder, the Monsignor mentions outside organisations, a possible second coming of Christ, and the Devil walking the earth." Bannerman bit his bottom lip slowly raising his eyes at the seeming absurdity of his last comments awaiting a reaction from his superior but there was none.

"You must find Gabriel Salmach, and report directly to me, do you understand?"

"Yes of course, sir," said Bannerman. "There is little more than thirty-six hours," continued the detective. Superintendent Blake looked at him inquisitively; Bannerman rose to his feet, before continuing, "Well, before the new millennium, that has to be the connection to where all this is leading. Sir, there was one thing, I did a check on Gabriel Salmach, didn't come up with much, his father worked for our government years ago, some kind of diplomatic go-between, but was mysteriously killed in a car accident in Austria, along with his wife. Only the child survived, been in and out of hospitals all his life, when I tried to dig further I just drew a blank, and certain doors, shall we say were slammed shut in my face."

Blake walked across towards the window, "Good work, Detective, we need to find him and draw some light on all this madness, I am convinced in some way he holds the key." The superintendent stared out across the narrow car park below. Bannerman thought of a paraplegic in a wheelchair having a connection with multiple killings of priests across the world, to be in some way preposterous, things still not adding up.

Bannerman walked across towards the door, "I will keep on it sir, and keep you updated with any findings." Blake remained silent, not turning from the window as the detective left the room.

Blake stood watching Bannerman and Sergeant Foster walk out across the car park. He just seemed to leer down in a perpetual trance, as if his gaze would dissect the vehicle they were about to climb into. Bannerman looked back up at the window, catching his superintendent's eyes which for a split second became locked.

The detective turned, opening the passenger door, climbing into the car. "You seem a bit tense Jack, are you alright?" asked Foster adjusting the driver's seat before switching the ignition into life. "Yeah..." He paused for a moment just staring up at the sky, "It seems Blake's being leaned on, yet why do I feel he's hiding something? This whole thing... that seems to be unravelling," he continued. "It cannot be true can it? My head tells me to remain on the rational side of the river, and expect an obvious solution, that's explicable, yet why am I so very scared?" Foster steered the car out through the gates.

Although it was early morning it felt unusually quiet, the silence felt almost palpable, to the point of eeriness.

Blake walked back towards his desk; he glanced down at the newspaper before smirking at the headlines and throwing it in the bin. He picked up the phone carefully pressing the numbers, putting the receiver against his ear as the ringing tone suddenly clicked.

"Once they have found the Christ, kill them both."

As the day moved on, the stillness remained as if the heart and circulation of the world had begun to wind down, almost to the point as if the very essence of life was slowly been drained away. Reports of strange occurrences began to filter through in daily news bulletins. In western South America, in Peru, the region of San Martin north of the country, the Huallaga River is one of the most important rivers in the region, forming together with its tributaries a "hydrographical system" that drains all of the surrounding territory. Yet for no apparent reason its waters suddenly turned a deep red... like blood. There were many other stories that seemed to get carried along with these sudden outlandish reported occurrences, a group of monks in an Italian monastery, Novalesa Abbey, awoke one morning all bearing "the five holy wounds" that was afflicted upon Jesus during the crucifixion.

Without any order people began to gather in and around places of worship; this compulsion began to spread, people just felt the need to pray and feel the essence of the Lord God. A vigil now gathered upon the Mount of Olives since the falling of rain that fell like blood. They came in vast numbers, their neighbours, their friends and their enemies alike. The mutual feeling of a miracle occurring was strong; people bowed and wept to the point of a growing hysteria as they refused to leave as the coming hour neared.

TWENTY-SEVEN

Nothing in his past was regarded sacred, no memories, the beginning of his life, his family, nothing. He cherished only what was to be, and what he would become within the world's new beginning. The ways of mankind had become tiresome to him; the world and life itself had long become predictable with an inevitable outcome that with order and restraint, man's abridgement to his freedom will only prolong what will be.

His thought process was channelled towards one goal, one eventuality and eternal power, within a world that would change forever, a new world that he welcomed. Although he manipulated a vast infrastructure within the government, and was a powerful instrument along the many corridors within this erratic "maze of power", yet he felt this position only stirred the ripples of the true depth of his destiny.

Jonathan Frazier had long awaited some greater being, some greater figure to follow beyond mere human expectations, dwelling within his ultimate anticipations. He had been chosen not to purely obey but to lead.

His father had always let it be known that like a dog he would obey throughout his life, "There are those who throw bones," he would say, "and there are those who fetch; you will always be dropping the bones at the feet of your superiors."

It had been a long time since he had heard those words; there was a nostalgic frown at the recollection, then a wide-eyed grin. He almost wished his father could stand before him once again and say them, his teeth clenched though still leering ahead at the thought of having to kill him again, as he had done many years ago.

Sir Reginald Frazier had been found dead, hung upside down burning from a tree in his garden; his head had been removed and stuck upon one of the posts at the side of his front gate. The killing went beyond his father's constant ridicule, and berating, beyond mere vengeance, this had been murder by necessity. Sir Reginald had stumbled upon something more sinister... a total evil spreading through a growing constraint within the boundaries of mere government jurisdiction. This underlying web of secrecy became the core of the infrastructure, becoming the body beneath the skin it portrayed. There had been a kind of irony by Sir Reginald's death at the hands of his son, as his father had always stated, "You could almost smell the thoughts and malicious nature of a killer, if you yourself are at one with him."

Jonathan Frazier had stood by the huge swirling hole, the darkness within turning as if growing outwards, almost to the point where it pulsated rhythmically as if exuding life within, like a pumping heart.

His anticipation heightened as he could sense the gathering deep inside, it moved towards the forefront and beyond. Although the constant screams and imploring for mercy that filtered across the opening did nothing to diminish his almost wanton urge to suppress these souls, to dwell in their perpetual torture, gleefully awaiting their tormentor. His body tingled as he felt the coming of those who would rule and give him the power he so relished.

This eventuality after the final hours when the gate would remain open forever, and the hosts of this infinite domain would pour forth at the feet of the one true God as he walks upon the earth in all his glory.

"The Christ has still not been found," the rasping voice seemed to circle him, as his shadow weaved across the room. He turned and bowed, "It is only a matter of time before one of them shall lead us to him, as your servants are everywhere." There was a slight trepidation; as he moved towards the figure that slowly began to emerge like a puff of smoke into the light, it was Cardinal Calvi.

"I do not exist by time," hissed the cardinal as he moved and shimmered before Jonathan Frazier. "Yet these dwindling hours are like the coming of my end." The small frame of the cardinal began to grow, shape changing, first to Abigail Tripp, whose fire-red eyes grew then fell away, as yet more hideous and grotesque creatures began stretching and pulling, screaming before yielding to their host who roared out in an unprecedented anger, while it turned from half-man and half-beast. Cardinal Calvi's hands slowly outstretched, gripping the side of the gateway, more images and souls condemned to this being seemed to evolve from in and around him.

Grotesque faces erupted from the stretching and breaking of skin and bone, the dark eyes of Maxim Wessler hovered upon his doll-like head as it jutted forward, hissing and shrieking as it reached out into the living world. Others lay defeated and horror-filled, screaming at their never-ending torture, their souls instilled within his command, each one ancient and new together. These souls trapped within an infinite domain of their own making, a prison of toil and suffering.

The cardinal's face began to split and fall away as it was just another disguise, another soul, bearing forth the inner core of evil. Jonathan Frazier's body tingled with both fear and exhilaration. He had welcomed the evils of the world, soaking within the pool of its allure, scouring the depths of its depravity, and long succumbing to its perpetual grip.

This ultimate host grew to its true form, lurching forward slavering and snarling in its grotesque entirety. This embodiment of terror drew power from the souls in and around him, and these souls were his, pledged to his will, for an eternity.

"The Christ is near I can feel him, I can taste his human flesh, find me the Christ, so that I may reign supreme forever..." hissing in his rage-like command, his two outstretched hands seemed to grow, the cartilage began breaking and reforming tendril-like. The stirring within the gateway grew into a fervent anticipation, almost to the point of an oncoming frenzy. Bodies began to emerge from the opening, oozing out across the floor snake-like, moving towards the host as if filled with a hunger only he could suppress. They slithered and writhed, becoming one, reaching to him in their pathetic dependency, yearning his acknowledgment, before being cast like grains of sand back into the abyss of their torment.

Silhouetted figures began to assemble, gathering in numbers forging together in a silent mass, awaiting the order of the Grand Master.

Jonathan Frazier's dark eyes scanned the gathering; his age-ing face bore no feeling, stirring no emotion, as he stared ahead almost trance-like. It was as if he was devoid of substance, or feeling. Emotion was something that dwelled within the weak, stirring some susceptible vulnerability that yielded to the human psyche, something he did not possess.

The host loomed before them, yet the mass that looked upon him, could only relish this penultimate evil with a blindness that was totally oblivious at not just the physical capabilities that he could bestow upon them. But the true damnation he would cast upon their souls if they failed him.

TWENTY-EIGHT

"No point avoiding it Jack," said Sergeant Foster, breaking the silence as they just sat in the car opposite the large grey building. Bannerman did not reply as he opened the car door and proceeded to walk across the street.

He had read somewhere that the treatment of inmates in early lunatic asylums was sometimes brutal, focussing on containment and restraint, whereas "modern psychiatric hospitals provide a primary emphasis on treatment, running along defined home office rules," yet containment and restraint were surely for the good of the patient. He approached the large ornate entrance, which loomed imposingly as it opened up into an arch before him. Bannerman felt his mouth run dry, this had been something that had always remained far away deep in the crevices of his mind, and it was something that happened to the unfortunates of life, something he need never associate with... until now.

He stood by the door staring at the brass plate Dr Herman J. Franks. Bannerman bowed his head before looking back at the car; Sergeant Foster nodded towards the door pointing his right forefinger. He waited inside the reception area before a small balding man approached; he moved with a prissy aloofness as he breezed across towards the detective. Bannerman stood as the doctor approached clutching a file that had his wife's name at the top.

"Good to see you Detective Bannerman," said the doctor opening the folder. For a moment he quickly scanned the pages nodding his head studiously like an officious bank clerk. "Has there been any change?" asked Bannerman trying to peer over the page.

"Let us step into my office," said Doctor Franks, pointing towards the middle of three doors along a short corridor.

The doctor sat down switching on the desk lamp placing the file before him. "You must understand, Detective," Doctor Franks steadied his glasses at the end of his nose as he peered across at Bannerman, "Your wife is suffering from psychiatric trauma, and this is in some way a normal response to an extreme event in her life, this being the death of your daughter." The doctor removed his glasses. "In lesser cases," he continued, crossing his fingers, "such trauma can be triggered by something as simple as a graphic media report, it in some way ignites a psychological reaction," he paused for a moment. "Your wife has essentially closed herself off to the surrounding reality of everyday life, as if in some way she is lingering within a self-imposed coma, and has... since the event created a series of emotional memories that are stored and structured deep within the brain."

"And how do we cure this psychiatric trauma?" asked Bannerman.

"Only time will tell, I am sorry if that sounds vague," replied the doctor. "She needs your love and support, and unfortunately all you can do is await the release from the psychological torment that has engulfed her." Bannerman watched Doctor Franks rise to his feet, "She continues to remain stable, but at this time she is still under the influence of sedatives, and up until recently she had shown little response to the treatment, yet she is sleeping more and has now started to eat; this is a positive sign Detective." Bannerman stood up, "Thank you doctor." He was almost relieved he did not have to see his wife, as she had been sedated, and on his last visit she did not recognise him, or worse her vacant stare was a look of choice, she had chose not to acknowledge he was there... it felt like a look of hate.

TWENTY-NINE

THE COMING OF THE DARKNESS

It is said the disclosure of future events lies like images through a dream, simple as pictures revealing the "end of age" as if in some way, that which will come to pass in the later days as the unveiling of revelations depicting God's way of dealing with humankind, when the living and the dead await the final judgement. Millennialism shall reveal separate destinies for the Christian church and Israel. The second coming, a one thousand year reign of "Messiah", a final test of the sinful nature of mankind by the coming of Satan, bearing a judgement of fire following the destruction of the current heaven and earth. Yet is God's ultimate purpose that which will create a new heaven and earth?

"Why is the sky turning black?" asked the little girl pointing as she stood beside the shop window with her mother. They both looked up in silence as vast strands of darkness began moving, linking together across the skyline, slowly spreading outwards vein-like, stretching like huge creepers upon a tree.

Ben Mills watched as the little girl and her mother began rushing down the street. "A storm is coming Ben, and we must prepare," said Gabriel Salmach, looking down at the boy. Ben somehow felt cocooned from the surroundings he found himself in, oblivious to the concern that was evident on the faces of the people nearby. He looked upon the sky as the fulminating mass evolved, as if growing, building into some great eruption that would reign down upon the world.

Several countries had reported the strange phenomena that seemed to be spreading across the world's skylines; as darkness began eerily moving towards the light of day, and in turn the light of day seemed to be decreasing in its intensity from the vicinity of the sun. It was welcomed with a heightened sense of hysteria, people of the world felt the essence of something coming that was both good and evil.

Maybe it had been fear, at first there were mass gatherings, people just standing staring above, some knelt and prayed; they anticipated it was a sign from God. Then the darkness began to grow, this only intensified the growing hysteria, people had already begun to swarm in large numbers, it was as if the oncoming revelation intensified their growing anxiety, those that chose to swarm in packs welcomed the darkness as if dancing to its allure with an unnatural glee, they could see opportunity and they were about to take it.

Bannerman and Sergeant Foster went to pick up Ethan Cole for questioning; they felt that he knew more than he was letting on, and nothing could be overlooked. Sometimes a doctor or nurse had a certain "bond" with a patient, a professional obligation for discretion, and a physiotherapist whose functions were physical intervention, and the constant promotion of mobility, which would take time, time to get to know the individual, gaining their confidence.

They pulled up by the small apartment block, and climbed out of the car. "What the…" said the sergeant staring up at the darkening sky. Bannerman said nothing as he just looked upon the gathering crowd that had congregated by the entrance and along the grass verge. The detective felt something fervent in the air that seemed to hang amongst the crowd, which had continued to thicken. Speckles of rain mixed with snow had begun to fall like tiny shards of glass amidst the gloom.

Bannerman could sense something changing in the atmosphere, and he did not like it. It was as if something was stirring within the mass of people, absorbing them. He continued to watch the darkness spreading, almost pulsating as it gathered en masse overhead. "This is seriously giving me the creeps Jack," said Foster slamming the car door shut.

"Yeah," said Bannerman, backing away from the car. "Let's find the physio and get out of here."

They began to make their way through the gathering crowd, towards the entrance when they noticed Ethan Cole standing there. "I was kinda expecting you guys," he said shaking the silver droplets out of his hair. The physiotherapist blew into his hands, raising his eyes above, "Man! I'm scared and I don't mind admitting it, these people just standing, staring, look at them! I can feel a mixture of fear and elation; it seems to be affecting them in different ways. Listen! Guys," he went on, "I gotta get to the Father, I can't explain why, I just got to go." There was a crashing sound as the breaking of glass shattered towards the rear of the crowd; they watched as a scuffle began to break out before the beginnings of a brawl ensued. "I think you're right Jack," said Foster, backing away towards the car. "Let's get the hell out of here!"

"What can you tell us about this...? Gabriel Salmach? It sounds foreign; his name that is," said Bannerman, studying Ethan in the rear-view mirror.

"Well... his files stated his father was Egyptian, mother was from right here in England, though you probably already know this, Gabe was a quiet kinda guy," replied Ethan.

"You are speaking of him in the past tense," said Sergeant Foster.

"You saw that place, the fire, sections of the hospital was completely destroyed; not much could have got out of there with two good legs, never mind a goddamn paraplegic." He paused for a moment, "I'm sorry I..." Ethan rubbed the sides of his forehead with both hands. Bannerman acknowledged him by nodding, he cared and the detective sensed this.

"I'd been his physio for just under a year," Ethan continued. "Not much to tell I guess. He had been paralysed after the car accident that killed his parents, and had suffered severe back trauma, for a long time he had given up ever walking again."

"Do you make them walk again, Ethan?" asked the sergeant, glancing over his shoulder.

"I'm here as a cushion, something for them to lean on, both physically and mentally. Only they can make themselves walk if at all possible, they have to want to and have the belief that they can. Look fellas," he went on. "All I know is, you got some fruitcake who has tried to burn down a hospital full of crippled men, women and children, don't you think you guys should be looking for whoever did this?"

"We think the fire, and the murdered priests could be in some way connected to Gabriel," replied Bannerman as he turned to face Ethan. "Connected, but how?" asked the physiotherapist shuffling in his seat, wide-eyed. "Come on guys, what are you suggesting – he wheeled himself out, murdered some priests? Got back in to the hospital and decided to burn it down."

There was a silence between the three men as they approached the dull outline of the church in the distance. The shrill sound of sirens filled the air, they watched as several groups of people who had began looting in shops, dispersed in all directions as police vans arrived screeching to a sudden halt. Bannerman stopped the car, an elderly woman stood in front of the vehicle staring curiously at them through the window. She began to walk around towards the driver's side. Sergeant Foster was about to let the window down, when she placed her two hands upon the glass; they watched as she leered at them before proceeding to run her tongue lasciviously along the outside of the driver's window. Foster leaned away in disgust, "What the fuck is wrong with her?" he asked clicking the door lock down. "You fucking son's of whores," she hissed, pounding against the glass, "He's coming, don't you see? He is fucking coming." Foster quickly turned the car almost knocking the woman down, she began screaming, chasing them; they looked upon the crowd who turned on the police response team. All they could do was watch as one of the officers was pulled from his vehicle, stripped almost naked, beaten and thrown straight through a shop window, while the remaining mob just rounded on the other officers. As the car sped away they thought they could hear screams, which very quickly diminished as the mob moved in.

The car picked up speed, the snow was now only faint as it fell in trickles, and although it stuck, the roads were awash with sleet and slush that sprayed continually against the underside of the car the faster it went. "Man, there is some weird shit going down here," said Ethan folding his collars around his neck, as he peered nervously up at the sky.

"The Father visited him a few times," he continued. "The last occasion he was kinda well... concerned."

"Why was that?" asked Bannerman, turning on the headlights as the darkness seemed to intensify by the second. *"These last remaining days and hours will prove to be the most important in human history."*

Monsignor Raffin's words presented themselves as if on a placard within his mind.

"Gabe was acting strange, started talking about the big guy upstairs," continued Ethan. Bannerman and Sergeant Foster looked at each other, and in turn glanced through the mirror at the physiotherapist.

"The almighty," said Ethan, sensing their confusion as he shrugged his shoulders pointing towards the roof of the car, his voice hushed. Bannerman was about to ask a question when his phone began to bleep in his inside pocket.

"Excuse me," he said turning towards Ethan, who just nodded as he continually stared nervously out of the window.

"Okay Charlie, slow down, there's a lot of crazy shit here too that I can't explain, now did you get that information for me?" The detective began to scribble something down in his notebook before slipping it inside his coat pocket, his eyes narrowing as he just shook his head.

"Sorry about that," said Bannerman, "just something I needed checking out. Did Gabriel say anything about dead priests?" The detective turned towards Ethan. "Hell no, he just seemed different, calmer, look! It can take a long time to come to terms with an injury like Gabe's, not walking and all. He just seemed at peace with himself," Ethan paused, shaking his head, again looking out of the car window. "The only way I can describe it... well, inside him there was a peace and understanding, yet it was much more than just coming to terms with his paralysis, like he had a sudden self-realisation that went beyond his predicament."

The darkness spread across the horizon, as if edging in and around the world, like some huge lid being forced across heaven itself.

"Thanks for your help, Ethan. Whatever reason all this is happening, I think soon will be revealed, at the end of this millennium."

The car drove across the gravel path through the gates of the church.

Father Creegan stood by the doorway of the rectory waving towards the car as it came to a stop.

Bannerman got out of the vehicle followed by his sergeant who opened the rear door for Ethan.

"Hey today is the last day of this century right?" Ethan asked, pulling the collars of his coat up and breathing in the cold air. "Man, I thought the winters were harsh back home in Philly, this is bleak as hell."

The priest looked upon Ethan with a concern in his eyes he could not hide, maybe it was the darkness looming across the daylight hours that made him start to shiver, or the decreasing temperature, or maybe the prophetic words that Ethan had just spoken, *"Bleak as hell."*

"Please come inside gentlemen," said the priest. He watched as thin vapours of darkness began to weave around the steeple of the church, these dark mists seemed to be looming down around the building's structure, slowly gathering.

They walked into the living room that was adequately lit; outside the dull twilight seemed to press upon the window at the opposite side of the room, dark shadows spiralled across the walls only to be broken by the soft flames of the fire. "I will go rustle up some coffee," said Ethan. The drab eerie stillness was interrupted by the frequent drone of sirens passing by, and people screaming and yelling, as they continued to gather in numbers.

"Does anybody know what is happening?" asked Bannerman, walking over towards the window. "Well Ethan is right," replied Father Creegan. "Today is the last day of the century and the start of a new millennium at midnight tonight; eleven priests have been slaughtered; on this eve I feel this is what these events are leading up to."

"Yeah, and if what that cardinal said is right we are talking hours before the crap hits the proverbial fan," said Sergeant Foster. "And I don't mind admitting, that I am really scared, I don't like this at all."

"Today when I awoke," continued Father Creegan, "there were people congregating outside and within the grounds of the church just standing in silent prayer."

"Or like they were in some kind of trance," said Foster. "The same thing seems to be happening everywhere, it's been on the news, some kind of phenomenon occurred near the holy city, seems to be stirring up mixed reactions."

"Yes the good and bad within us shall bear forth," said the priest. "And the evil will fight hard to win."

Bannerman remained reticent by what he inwardly continued to ignore although his gut feeling remained in overdrive. "This darkness outside seems to be thickening," he said, peering out at the silhouette of the church across the graveyard. He quickly moved closer, arching his hand against the glass, there was something out there. "Looks like you got a visitor Father," said the detective turning to face the priest, who began to walk towards him frowning.

"Visitor, what are you talking about Jack?"

"There is some kid stood in your churchyard, and he seems to be coming towards the house."

Father Creegan leaned towards the window squinting. He watched as what appeared to be a boy moving as if he was drifting across the darkness towards them.

Bannerman walked towards the door, quickly opening it; the boy just stood upon the grass barefoot and shivering, the detective proceeded to run outside.

"Come on in, kid, you're sure not dressed for these conditions." He removed his coat placing it around the boy's shoulders, "Let's get you indoors."

Foster moved a chair closer to the fire; they watched as the boy just sat down staring blankly into the flames.

"What you doing out there, son? Want to catch your death," asked the sergeant shaking his head looking down at the boy's wet bare feet; he continued to shiver staring at the crackling flames of the fire.

Ethan Cole walked into the room backing the door open as he carried a tray of hot drinks; he turned to place the tray on the small table at the side of the fire when he suddenly gasped; standing upright the tray fell from his hands as he keeled over falling hard against the bureau.

At first everybody in the room just stopped and stood still, the boy leapt up from the chair towards where Ethan lay, and began weeping, pulling at him.

Bannerman gripped the boy ushering over his sergeant for help.

"Ethan, are you alright? What's wrong?" asked Bannerman kneeling beside him. The detective placed a cushion under his head, gently slapping the side of his face.

"Father I think he needs something stronger than coffee."

The priest rushed towards his desk pulling a half-empty bottle of whisky from the drawer; he proceeded to pour it into a glass, almost filling it halfway before handing it to the detective.

"Come on Ethan, drink some of this," said Bannerman, tilting the physiotherapist's head up slightly. Ethan stirred, moving his head from side to side, he began to gurgle and wretch as the detective slowly poured a portion of the liquid down his throat.

"Looks like he doesn't like your whisky either," said Bannerman, handing the glass back to the priest.

For a few moments, Ethan stirred uneasily before his eyes slowly began to open, he was breathing heavily; although he lay uncomfortable, he appeared calm.

Bannerman leaned back looking at the others as Ethan started to weep; at first covering his face, shaking his head, before moving his hands revealing two large round moist eyes confused and scared, yet twinkling amidst the glow of the fire as tears fell down his cheeks.

"What is it Ethan?" asked the priest, kneeling beside him, gripping his hand, as he slowly began to rise up. "What's wrong?"

"Is it you? Is it truly you Ben?" The boy crouched beside the physiotherapist placing his hand upon his shoulder.

"Yes," he replied, smiling across at Ethan who continued to cry as he reached out clutching the boy tightly.

"We are all a little confused here Ethan," said Bannerman as he helped him to his feet. Ethan staggered slightly before being placed in a chair.

"You know this kid?" continued Bannerman, nodding towards the boy.

"Sure, this is Ben Mills, the young guy I was telling you about," he replied. "He was well…" Ethan gathered his thoughts before continuing, "Clinically dead, kept alive because of his organs." He made no reaction to the absurdity of his comments.

Sergeant Foster walked across towards the desk and poured himself a large drink.

"What you are saying, that this boy was a patient at St Michael's?" asked Bannerman frowning.

"There is not much time," said Ben. "He awaits you in the church."

Father Creegan walked across towards the boy placing a hand upon his shoulder, "Ben, who awaits us?" he asked, even though his anticipation was heightened by the boy's words.

Bannerman beckoned the priest over towards the window. "Listen, Father, before we go in there, the cardinal we met at the church, well… the Monsignor informed me he was already dead, I mean…" he paused before continuing, "I did a check, and he had been killed in mysterious circumstances, that's all the Vatican were prepared to say, that was almost two weeks ago."

"Yes," said the priest, "The Devil will take many forms for his own ends, but I feel it is not the cardinal who awaits us."

Glass from the window by the door suddenly exploded into the room, as the projectile crashed against the wall. "There are people gathering at the edge of the graveyard," Sergeant Foster shouted, pointing across through the hole in the window. They watched as the dark silhouettes of the crowd at first seemed to just stand in silence, then they slowly began to move towards the house.

"Gentlemen, I feel we must go now!" said the priest, his expression held a look of fear that seemed to pale his complexion.

Other objects thudded against the walls of the rectory. "Let's go, now!" yelled Bannerman. They ran towards the entrance of the church, the detective quickly forced the door open ushering them inside. He watched for a moment as figures moved as if like carvings from the darkness, hovering against the gloom.

"I could hear you in the dark," said Ben, "and there were times within my sleep I could see you," he continued, turning towards the physiotherapist. "I could see you looking upon me, Ethan. I felt your grief and pain, and I did not feel alone in the darkness, thank you for being there."

Ethan began to weep again, clutching the boy tightly. "I can't believe it's really you Ben." He began to rub his eyes with his sleeve, "You are never going in no dark place again, I promise you, old Ethan will see to that."

The priest for a moment stood inside the entrance, his eyes blinked nervously as he began scanning the interior, he was drawn towards the burning candles, their flames rippled as if scurrying across the edge of the pews like a sudden spew of butterflies. The others just stood in the foreground, as he walked across towards the central isle before kneeling down and making the sign of the cross. He stood and looked upon the outline of the figure in the distance kneeling at the far side of the altar, just staring upon the cross above the altar table in silence. The priest's hands had begun to shake.

Father Creegan slowly walked towards the man; he was aware his heart began to thump hard in his chest, a mixture of fear, hope and anticipation began to overwhelm him with each step he took.

THIRTY

The priest continued to walk towards the altar, the trepidation he felt seemed to orchestrate his movements, feeling compelled to almost tiptoe as he neared what was to become real before him, as the figure slowly turned around to face him.

"Is it you? Is it really you, Gabriel? But I... you," Father Creegan's words became jumbled as he knew what he could see and witness, yet his mind's rational doors all slammed shut at once; at something it was incapable of conceiving.

Gabriel Salmach stood before the priest and smiled. Father Creegan slumped back upon the bench and for a moment just said nothing. All he could do was look upon a man who stood in the midst of his church, no longer incapacitated by his physical burdens; he looked upon a man who stirred the very confines of his belief and faith, in all that he represented and preached.

"I am what you see Father," said Gabriel, as he lay out his hands. "Like you, I stand upon the world as flesh and blood, amidst mankind's interpretations of this advent, this Parousia or epiphany, in which he chooses to believe by the strength of his faith, 'this second coming'." For a moment he just looked above, "But at this time I stand before you as a man, my coming was through the natural process of humanity, my epiphany was to be born once again, to live among you, dwelling in your greed and hatred, to suffer in your pain, and to live by your imperfections. I need your faith and belief this night, to protect me; the evil of mankind is strong, and my vulnerability is susceptible, as forces from the dark move swiftly towards us in these final hours."

Bannerman and Sergeant Foster slowly made their way around the outside aisle towards the altar.

"But you have come back among us, is it not to save us?" asked the priest.

"You have the capabilities to save yourself," replied Gabriel. "Within your belief," he went on, "as believers shall drive out evil in the name of God."

Father Creegan recognised the familiarity in his words; they were from the Gospel according to Mark.

"You once said the Bible is full of inaccuracies, yet you choose to preach it?" Again Gabriel smiled at the priest, "I preach only the true word of God," he replied.

The priest noticed his eyes shone with an exuberance, which seemed unrestrained as if he absorbed all things around him. "Your questions shall be answered by your faith in God the Father," Gabriel continued.

"Excuse me Father," interrupted Bannerman as he walked between the two men. "Mr Salmach we need to speak with you." Gabriel Salmach turned towards the detective.

"Your belief has been weakened in your refusal to accept the will of God," said Gabriel.

"Wrong, pal! My belief is in the law, and we need to talk about some dead priests. I thought this guy was paralysed?" said Bannerman, turning towards the priest, who did not answer.

"Gabe... my God is that you?" asked Ethan, wide-eyed as he stood beside Ben at the rear of the church. Gabriel smiled as he turned to face Ethan who began to rush up the aisle towards him.

"Yes it is I..." said Gabriel, as he walked down towards Ethan open armed.

"Man this is too much for me," said the physiotherapist as they hugged. "Holy sh... your legs, you got legs, I mean you can walk," he said pointing to Gabriel's legs in disbelief.

* * *

"Excuse me gents, I don't know what's going on here," continued Bannerman, "but Mr Salmach you have some explaining to do."

"Your faith is in you, all you need is guidance to find it," said Gabriel.

175

Bannerman could feel the anger surge within him. "Look we are not here for a sermon, whatever else is supposedly going on, there are still two murders to be solved."

"Please take my hand," asked Gabriel as he extended his arm to the detective. Bannerman looked around at the expectant faces of the others, who just stood by in silence. "Be careful Jack," whispered Sergeant Foster.

Jack Bannerman walked towards Gabriel frowning. "Okay pal, you got me," he said, gripping his hand. "Come and walk with me," replied Gabriel smiling. For a moment Jack Bannerman was standing within the darkened interior of the church, when suddenly he was stood amidst what looked like an operating theatre in a hospital. He looked around the room; a sterile odour pricked his nostrils as he watched a physician and his assistant standing by a bed, both in moisture-proof gowns. The screams of the woman being attended had a familiarity... it was his wife.

Bannerman looked beyond the physician and the midwife upon the face of his wife who was about to give birth to their daughter. Familiar feelings began to flutter through him, feelings he had felt at the first shrill screams of his daughter as she entered the world.

Like the flicking of pages, the days and months passed by in seconds; he witnessed images and events of his life, which were shared by them all as a family. He was suddenly distracted as a fierce breeze blew around him, the leaves upon the ground stirred and sprayed out upon the bleak autumn daylight. He watched as they walked through a park, he looked upon himself as he picked up bundles of the leaves, and playfully scattering them upon the pram, as the little girl screamed with laughter, while they slowly drifted down upon her as she reached out her small arms to catch them. He looked upon the scene that began to drift away, a sudden weight within his heart stirred as he looked around at the distant surroundings; they were surroundings he wanted to pull back and stay within, but like a rolling mist, it just came and went.

Then came the illness; he watched her rosy cheeks begin to pale, as time continued, to wither away; he felt helpless as he could only watch her dying before his eyes.

He had remembered how he begged and pleaded with God. Bannerman began to fight, to force himself back to what was real, but all he could do was witness the deterioration of his daughter… and eventually witness her death. The bitterness that was there burned within him once more stirring his anger.

"All things that come to pass are within the will of God," said Gabriel. Bannerman shielded his damp eyes from the light that poured from above where they were stood.

"Push me Daddy, push me."

He looked around within his surroundings that continued to shimmer before him. The detective tried to find reason to what he was witnessing, like he was caught within some eerie drug-induced dream sequence that was forced upon him. *"Push me Daddy, push me."* "Ashley!" he screamed out, "Ashley where are you?" The brightness became more intense, he shielded his eyes, the light sprayed across the back of his hands and through his fingers, yet something was moving beyond. The detective's eyes began to blink against the brightness, he looked through as it began to disperse, and he could see the little girl in the distance moving from side to side.

For a moment he just stood as the familiar scene before him became clear, Ashley was sat on a swing like the one he had made for her in their garden, with some rope and an old wooden fence plank.

"Push me Daddy, push me," she yelled.

Bannerman rushed towards his daughter, wanting to hold her, to cling to her. "Oh sweetheart, I miss you so much," he began to weep uncontrollably. "Daddy loves you, you know that don't you?" Her spirit stood before him.

"Yes Daddy but Mummy needs you, you need to go to her and bring her from the dark place, she's sad and very lonely; she needs you Daddy."

The detective knelt before the child, blinking against the trickling tears in his eyes.

"Okay baby, Daddy will promise," he said staring into her soft blue eyes as she smiled at him.

"Push me Daddy, push me."

Bannerman stood pushing his daughter on the swing, it moved slowly through the air, his daughter laughing.

"Remember I will always be in your dreams Daddy." Her voice seemed to resonate across the air, as the swing did not return and the light began to fade. "No! Ashley," Bannerman yelled, reaching out his hand. "Please... come back." But the darkness seemed to fold around the remaining light, and she was gone. He was back in the church clutching Gabriel's hand. "Who... what are you?" he asked, breathing hard in continued short bursts, as he rubbed his eyes looking around for any lingering trace of his daughter, but there was none. "The clarity is not what you see before you," said Gabriel. "The clarity is what you feel in your heart, and what you will continue to feel all the days of your life. Ashley will be with you always."

The detective gripped the edge of a pew, as he tried to gather his thoughts; he looked around at the others who seemingly studied him in confused curiosity, their stare was one of indifference... like nothing happened.

"How long was I gone?" he asked turning towards Sergeant Foster, the sergeant frowned puzzled.

"Gone where Jack? You never left the church."

Jack Bannerman looked over at Gabriel Salmach, who just smiled back.

"Hey you guys, I don't mean to break up the party," said Ethan. "But there's a whole bunch of people outside with hoods on, and believe me, that's never a good sign."

For a few moments the silence seemed perpetuated by an inward expectancy as they turned looking at the rear of the church. The darkness spread as the candle stands at the corners of the entrance seemed to shake and vibrate across the floor before toppling over. Suddenly like stills from a film, the doors of the church were literally blown inwards with such force; each door seemed to just crumble into fragmented pieces, and was sent crashing against the walls and ceiling, before falling down against the pews before them.

One by one the large oval ornate windows shattered from side to side splintering inwards, fine shards of glass seemed to rip into the looming darkness exploding against the walls, before being sucked back into the night.

The candle stands by the altar were blown over; one fell against a side curtain sending ripples of flames to spread across the surface, before moving unnaturally across the walls and floor, like thin aluminous veins.

Ethan Cole gripped Ben around the shoulders, ushering him towards the far end of the altar, they proceeded to duck down beside the confession box where the others were hiding behind the front side pews.

The fire continued to move around the Eucharist as if its inward motive was to encircle them and close in like some deadly embrace.

Bannerman could only stand and watch as several hooded figures had begun running through the entrance of the church. He watched as the darkness poured in with them, at first lingering and joining together, gathering en masse, it turned in mid-air slowly evolving... as if it had purpose.

The detective ran across the centre aisle in turn blocking the path as one of the hooded figures ran menacingly towards him. He watched as the figure pulled out a large knife and proceeded to thrash out, catching him on the arm. Bannerman felt the searing pain as blood began to trickle inside his jacket across his skin; he felt it running down towards his clenched fist.

The detective grabbed the top of his assailant's robe pulling him across a wooden pew, forcing him off balance, and in turn reaching towards the rim of his hood quickly pulling it towards the opposite direction with a fierce "jerk" he felt something snap as the man fell limply to the floor.

Another figure ran towards Sergeant Foster, now driven on pure adrenalin, he instinctively picked up a nearby candle holder quickly swinging it towards the man's legs; the figure crashed against a wall where the fire had dangerously begun to spread moving down upon a nearby curtain. The sergeant watched as the rim of the man's robe began to burn, the fire was like some raging animal, agile, impartial, as it quickly began to engulf him, the material of the robe began to crackle and burn... maybe it was the man's skin, thought the sergeant as he quickly turned away ignoring the muffled screams.

More of these hooded figures began to pour through the entrance.

"We are not going to hold this lot off, Jack, there's too many of them," said Foster backing up the aisle. Bannerman picked up an ornate candle stand that stood at the side of the altar swinging hard against the head of a second attacker, the impetus of the blow sent him crashing across the altar falling awkwardly against the central rail, the man fell limply like some doll-like parody, submissively in his instant death.

The darkness began to move around them, encircle them, weaving nonchalantly around the altar, yet still growing outwards. Bannerman thought he could hear faint noise, seemingly coming from within its growing depth.

Suddenly the hooded figures stopped where they stood, just spreading across the bottom of the church... waiting.

Bannerman and the others just stood and watched as a lone figure appeared at the church entrance, before slowly walking up the central aisle. Bannerman rose to his feet. He squinted; studying the man, there was a familiarity as he came closer.

"Find the boy and kill him," he yelled.

Ethan Cole moved to the edge of a pew. "Listen Ben, when I give you the signal I want you to run towards the vestry over there," he pointed towards a passageway that forked towards the right of the altar. "You got that?" The boy nodded.

Two hooded figures ran across the end aisle near where Ethan and Ben crouched.

"Now Ben, go!" yelled Ethan, as he stood and proceeded to charge at the two oncoming assailants.

Ethan ran towards his oncoming attackers, buffeting them with his bulk, sending one of them sprawling across the floor, before the other fell so hard against the edge of a free-standing column he was knocked unconscious.

Father Creegan's vision hung fragmented, like some surreal sprinklings from a kaleidoscope turning before him. He felt blood trickle down the side of his head from a gash; minutes had disappeared as he looked around confused. The priest gripped the altar rail as he struggled to get to his feet; his legs would not move, as he just slumped against the floor, his vision began to fall into place, he looked towards where Gabriel had been stood, but he was no longer there... he was gone.

THIRTY-ONE

THE COMING OF THE LIGHT

Jonathan Frazier walked across and knelt beside the priest, gripping his head as he held a large knife across his throat. "Father... where is your God?" he asked, sniggering in the direction of the detective who was slowly edging towards him. "Where is the Christ? Look around you, these pathetic images, and these flagrant narcissistic idols you choose to worship." He laughed, pointing the knife towards the crucifix, "Let me tell you," he continued, his face tightening. "Very soon you shall witness the one true God." Bannerman ran towards the priest but was apprehended by several hooded figures as they began to gather around him, he could only stand and watch as the rest of the hooded mass proceeded to tear the church apart; Sergeant Foster and Ethan were led to the altar.

The looming darkness seemed to fulminate, turning like evolving puffs of smoke as it began forming, and circling before being sucked in and re-emerging upon itself.

The voices seemed distant at first, garbled hollow tones, before the apparent screams and pleading had begun to reach the forefront of the now emerging hole that protruded from the belly of the darkness like an eerie grin.

Bannerman edged backwards as the noise from within the gathering mass began to vibrate louder, so loud the Stations of the Cross fell down from the wall, exploding across the floor. The pews began to vibrate and shift, scraping along the floor as they thudded up and down.

"I will not ask again, where is the Christ and the boy?"

"Where the hell is Gabriel Salmach?" asked Bannerman looking over at the bewildered priest, Jonathan Frazier glared at the detective, the recognition in the name seemed to startle him, and Bannerman noticed this.

Jonathan Frazier pointed at his men who apprehended Ethan; they proceeded to drag him towards the Grand Master. Ethan pulled against his captors; one punched him fiercely below the ribs forcing him to keel over. Bannerman watched as he was dragged towards the edge of the altar. "Where is your God, when you most need him?" laughed Jonathan Frazier as he gripped Ethan around the throat, there was a moment's pause before he swiftly plunged the knife deep into his chest.

"Ethan no!" screamed the detective. Bannerman kicked out at one of his captors sending him reeling over the altar rail, as he proceeded to run towards the physiotherapist.

Ethan groaned, before slowly dropping to his knees, a fine line of blood began to roll down the side of his mouth, and his eyes turned inwards as he fell forward.

Bannerman quickly knelt beside the stricken physiotherapist, carefully turning him over, before placing his hand behind his head slowly raising it up. "We need an ambulance for this man, now!" he yelled, his voice quivering in anger and panic. Blood began to haemorrhage from the wound; Ethan blinked wearily looking up at the detective. "Hang on in there Ethan, you will be okay," said Bannerman, pressing his hand against the wound to try and stem the blood as it now oozed out across the back of his fingers. Ethan gripped the detective's forearm, "Ta… take care of the little guy," he coughed, spluttering fine droplets of blood across his face. "I promised him," he continued, "I promised him he would never be alone… take care of… Ben."

Bannerman and the others could only watch as Ethan's eyes slid shut; at first his body shook before slumping against the stone floor in silence. Amidst everything before them, the total surreal events of the situation that presented itself seemed unprecedented in its contradiction, by what began to proliferate from the opening. Yet anger burned within the detective, he knew the priest and his sergeant would be next, and he had to act quickly.

The hole continued to spread across the back of the altar, its depth turning, as if moving in upon itself. He watched, almost captivated, as at first the many images which spawned from it. Faces, hollow and gaunt, slavering grotesquely as they appeared upon the surface of the hole, their sunken eyes blinking away the darkness as if reborn, yet they seemed compelled by a yearning, an imploring that hovered within the restraint of their doomed souls. The young girl from the hospital, her hypnotic gaze fixed upon the detective, for a moment he thought he could see a flicker of life... flickers of recognition.

Suddenly the distorted features of Cardinal Calvi jutted forward, his head tight almost skeletal; his being began to shimmer, changing, remoulding into many grotesque caricatures that pulsated, vibrating as the continued roars from within seemingly forced outwards by whatever was making its way to the surface.

Sergeant Foster and the priest were knocked of their feet as the vibrations from within grew in their intensity. Suddenly the beast began to reach the forefront; this unprecedented evil began to almost tear its way into the world.

Maxim Wessler emerged, he stretched, yelling out, his shrill-like screams forced from his cadaverous emaciated body that began to wriggle pathetically, as it fell from the host, crawling across the floor like a huge scavenging insect.

Bannerman noticed Father Creegan kneeling, his eyes closed; he clasped the crucifix around his neck, hands trembling as he prayed. More infernal creatures came through the gateway, demonic monsters hovering in mid-air, wings snapping out from their bulbous backs rasping harshly like repetitive abrasive groans.

The beast roared out in a continued outburst, its anger unsuppressed, as it emerged growing in stature; its talons rose as if scraping across the darkness, hovering before the detective who began to back away from the huge circular entrance.

Bannerman shook his head; he felt the urge to almost laugh out loud at the absolute helplessness that befell them. "Please, we need you," he yelled, as he looked around the church in desperation. "We need you, please Lord God, we need you now."

The imploring and desperation in his voice trailed across the air only to be met by the shrill laughter of Jonathan Frazier, who walked defiantly towards the edge of the altar.

"Call out to your God, I pity you," he hissed. "For he will not come," he went on, shaking his head. "This is your God." He pointed towards the beast that loomed before the detective. The opening continued to move outwards, it was as if it would devour everything and everyone around it.

"Kneel! Before the one true God," commanded Jonathan Frazier. "Do it now."

The detective frowned hard at the Grand Master. "The one true God is about to return and destroy you and these monsters that you worship," he replied. "Gabriel Salmach shall destroy you all." Bannerman watched as Jonathan Frazier clenched his teeth wide-eyed, clutching the knife as he began to move towards him, it was what Bannerman had anticipated, and he waited for his chance. He ran towards him as he descended the altar steps, leaping feet first, catching the Grand Master full in the chest with enough force to send him reeling backwards, towards the mouth of the opening.

Bannerman watched as Jonathan Frazier stumbled, still clutching the knife; for a moment he hovered unable to hold his balance. The detective ran towards him gripping him by the wrist, and without any hesitation struck the Grand Master hard in the face; he quickly turned him round by the arm pressing the knife against his back, and proceeded to grip him around the throat. "This is for Ethan," said Bannerman as he quickly forced the knife up between his shoulder blades. The detective stood and watched as the Grand Master yelled out as he staggered forward trying to pull out the knife from his back. He fell to his knees before slumping against the entrance as he was being sucked in towards the gateway and seemed to claw desperately at the air. He glared back at the detective, looking upon a world he despised. Bannerman rushed forward throwing him towards an abyss he seemed to crave. Jonathan Frazier would fall to his death screaming, maybe the last remnants of humanity forced the stark realisation of where he would remain for his own eternity. The beast roared out moving towards Bannerman.

Ben Mills slowly walked towards the edge of the centre aisle, just standing silently with his hands by his sides.

"Get back kid!" said Bannerman, as he looked upon this strange young child who just stood defiant before the beast. The outside darkness that was forged against the very structure of the church slowly began to dispel as faint streams of light poured through its depth.

This sudden spray of light seemed to pour across towards where the boy was stood, and then slowly it began to move upon the aisles and pews, edging across the walls and columns within the church. Bannerman shielded his eyes as the light became more intense. He noticed the outline of a figure walking through the now brilliant, seemingly aluminous, avalanche forging its presence through the centre. Ben Mills turned towards it and bowed, it was Gabriel Salmach.

The beast moved towards the boy, its head jutting forward slavering in anticipation as it was about to strike him, Ben still did not move.

Gabriel stood within the forefront of the light; his outstretched hands emitted a glowing sphere that covered the beast, engulfing it, forcing it backwards. It screamed out as it struggled within the glow that had now begun to move upwards, falling across the creatures that hovered above.

There seemed to be a surge of activity taking place outside the church, as a mass of scuffles broke out, the hooded followers that were guarding the entrance were being attacked.

The light continued to move across the winged creatures, it sprayed down upon the rest of the hooded followers that just stood in silence across the aisles.

"Look!" yelled Sergeant Foster, pointing above. One by one the flying monsters began to burst into flames, as they just seemed to crumble and explode in mid-air. The same began to happen as the continued cadaverous bodies emerged from the gateway, crawling and slavering before groups of flames began to spill across them, engulfing them. Ben turned, stepping to the side as he lined the path awaiting Gabriel as he slowly walked forward. The brilliance of the light seemed to exasperate the beast that roared, hissing as it glared down at them.

THIRTY-TWO

"Let me taste your flesh," it screamed, moving towards Gabriel. Bannerman beckoned his sergeant to take cover as he ran towards Father Creegan, gripping him by the arm, ushering him behind a column at the rear of the altar. The beast began to force the structure of the church to vibrate, shuddering as it began to crumble inwards.

The remaining pews were suddenly ripped up crashing against the sides of the walls, smashing in pieces across the floor. They watched as the altar split in two before falling inwards as the ground began to shift, emitting flames that scurried across the surface moving outwards towards each corner of the building. The violent screams of the host roared amidst the mayhem and destruction as it rushed towards Gabriel who just seemed to rise within the brilliant glow that now completely surrounded him, suppressing the looming darkness, forcing it back towards the gateway.

Gabriel's spiritual prominence rose up as the brilliant sheen of light continued to emanate from his outstretched hands. The darkness that had been forged against the church and beyond now seemed to split and fall away as if melting.

The hooded figures that had surrounded Sergeant Foster and the priest had now begun to flee towards the entrance. The glare of the beast seemed to stop them, rendering them in mid-movement. The beast's eyes flashed a blood-red, hate-filled, intensifying its concentration, roaring towards these traitors, its talons spread outwards as if summoning them back. The hooded figures for a moment did not move, until one by one their piercing screams broke the silence as they began tearing at their robes as if excruciating pain was surging through their bodies.

The continued shrill screams resonated an imploring within them.

"What's going on Jack?" asked his sergeant confused, peering above an overturned bench covering the central aisle.

Bannerman shook his head, saying nothing; all he could do was look on in silence.

The hooded mass continued to thrash out wildly, a thin vapour rising from the top of their robes. Gathering and forming in mid-air like puffs of smoke, as one by one they began to drop where they stood. Although the vapour had no solidity, it took shape forming from the bodies it poured from, reforming into them, it was their souls summoned forth by the beast that now owned them, extracted from their human remains that just fell like crumpled sheets against the floor.

Their souls continued to gather in mid-air all bearing one common possession, FEAR. Bannerman and the others could only watch as the mass of souls forged together as they became drawn towards the gateway, and the realisation that became etched against their silent distorted faces went beyond their fear. They had orchestrated their own destiny that was to be their end without an end.

The beast once again began to distort and shape change; it began to grow outwards its talons drawing the structure of the church to shudder and crumble, and cracks began to open across the walls, moving up towards the apex of the roof. "We need to get out of here," shouted Sergeant Foster. "No wait!" said Father Creegan. "Don't you see?" he said rising to his feet, pointing towards Ben Mills. "He has been chosen to line the path as an Apostle of the Lord, Ben has been chosen, he is the last of the twelve, and he is protected by God."

Masonry from the roof began to fall down, and large segments of the walls started to crumble inwards as the beast continued to grow before them. "Look! Jack," said the sergeant pointing towards the church entrance. Bannerman watched as Monsignor Raffin stood in the doorway making the sign of the cross, as groups of cardinals gathered around him.

They watched as the monster before them continued to grow disproportionately, huge wings snapping out from its back. The evil within was unsurpassed, boundless as like a huge coil it continued to unravel, like some endless spillage drowning out the glimmer of good that stood in its way.

Yet within the ferocity of this "being" there seemed to be vulnerability, like some awareness within stirring its fear. This beast has entered God's created world, bestowing all temptation upon mankind's susceptibility to commit sin, and in this, his power would remain absolute. Some "infernal beings" still lingered overhead, dwelling in the slow diminishing darkness before succumbing to the light, the "essence of God" that continued to flourish throughout the church.

"You will return to your abyss," said Gabriel. The beast emitted a ball of fire. Gabriel slowly brought his hands together, as the fireball rushed towards him; it split in two before diminishing to nothing.

"It is the will of God you will now return," he said, as his spiritual prominence continued to hover before the beast. Monsignor Raffin and several cardinals began to kneel at the edge of the aisles; the Islamic imam walked forward, and knelt beside the Monsignor, followed by an elderly Rabbi who for a moment seemed almost awestruck as he shuffled to the forefront. The imam rose to his feet aiding the Rabbi to kneel. They in turn bowed their heads in their own silent prayer.

The beast continued to shape change, more infernal messengers began to emerge, and these dark angels had walked the earth within society's hierarchy, in many instances existing as leaders of man. And angels both good and bad, are something man has an inability to distinguish, thus permitting the existence of this devil.

The light poured around the beast, rendering it, forcing it back towards the gateway; for a moment it just looked across at Gabriel. "I shall always walk upon your precious world, I am a perpetual guest of these pathetic mortals, as they cannot help themselves, I will always thrive because of their hate and greed towards each other. I will always exist because of them," it continued. Abigail Tripp stood before Gabriel, her head tilted, pointing towards him smiling. "Within the will you have given them, they shall always walk towards the darkness; this preference is fuelled by their ignorance, it is what they choose."

The beast stood before the now spinning gateway in its human form, continually changing, into recognisable figures, earthly rulers, these "infernal angels" of the dark knew no restrictions, their presence upon the living world was to influence and lead, yet within their new world regime, they were dwellers of the abyss, messengers of the Devil.

Abigail Tripp walked towards the opening which now begun to spin around her, an avalanche of evil surged within her innocent human form, as once again the beast emerged in its entirety, it roared out as it fell backwards, falling through the gateway amidst continued roars and screams.

The gateway continued to spin, swirling in mid-air, the remaining strands of darkness were sucked in towards it, before the screams and roars had begun to diminish and fade, until a surge of fire began to circle, burning across the opening until it faded to nothing.

They stood and watched as the last flickers of the gateway disappeared, leaving an eerie undertone against the stillness of the church.

THIRTY-THREE

Bannerman and his sergeant emerged from the debris, and for a moment they just stood in silence not knowing what to say or do.

Monsignor Raffin walked forward; the overwhelming look in his eyes caused his hands to tremble as he slowly joined them together.

The other religious dignitaries gathered around the Monsignor before kneeling, some began to weep, tears flowing amidst the wonderment within their eyes.

Gabriel Salmach walked forward towards the edge of the light that continued to pour through the church, his spiritual prominence shone, yet he began to change, back to flesh and blood.

He stood within the silence as the gathering just looked upon him. "The words spoken by the evil one," said the Monsignor, "are the shortfalls of mankind, please guide us." Monsignor Raffin knelt before Gabriel bowing. "Your existence is given to you from God," he replied, looking down upon the Monsignor. "Your continuity, and destiny," he continued, "is shaped by your own hands." Gabriel began to walk around the gathering, "Your freedom of choice is as essential to your make up as the blood that flows through your veins. There are many beliefs among us," he went on. "You choose to pray and worship a 'higher being' within your cultures. I am not here to preach if that is right or wrong, what is important is the acceptance of one who is deemed the almighty, the essence of the light that pours around these walls, is the essence of God the creator of all you see. He is perceived in many forms, but you must remember there is only one God, one creator of life." Gabriel walked back towards the forefront. "I have been born onto this world

192

of flesh and blood, bestowed with your emotions, your fear and pain, dwelling within your vulnerability, and susceptible to the sin of all man. But within this great creation that inhabits this world, I found the human heart such a powerful instrument, as it is the source of all life, it harbours love and forgiveness, as it does compassion for your fellow man." Gabriel raised his arms staring above, "If you are to walk forever within the kingdom of God, first you must embrace the culture and creed of each other; dwell within boundaries but do not close them off. Quite simply you are not the innkeeper of lands of your own choosing, but merely an inhabitant within God's creation. Its geographical advantages are to be shared not hoarded for profit." He looked upon the gathering dignitaries, "The evil that you witnessed dwells upon hatred and sin; it exists because these emotions within your hearts allow it to. Search deep within your spirit, do not let fear and hatred suppress the love that God has given you, and the answers you search for will become much clearer to his will." Gabriel looked over towards Bannerman smiling. "There is something I must do before I leave."

Gabriel walked across to where Ben Mills was crouched sobbing beside Ethan's body.

He placed his hand upon the boy's shoulder, smiling down at him; he beckoned him over to stand by him. They both looked upon Ethan in silence.

Ben continued to cry, "Why did he have to die?" He ran the back of his hand across his eyes. "Everybody who ever cared for me is dead," he said.

"Ben, you have been brave beyond your young years," replied Gabriel. "And through all the years of your life I will watch over you, as shall Ethan." Ben looked towards Gabriel, the soft running tears dripping from his eyes. Gabriel moved towards the physiotherapist, crouching before him, slowly placing his hand upon Ethan's forehead. "Awaken Ethan." His words seemed to trail across the air, their command absolute, and the finality of their request lingered against the silence. The gathering seemed to move closer. At first there was nothing until a slight flicker in his left leg.

"Oh my G…" said Sergeant Foster, backing away towards the altar almost falling over what was left of the rail. The sergeant held his mouth, as he began to whimper. Bannerman shook his head in disbelief stumbling backwards before falling to his knees.

Ethan's fingers began to twitch and shake, stretching out. There were gasps from the gathering. Father Creegan walked over, kneeling beside the physiotherapist gripping his hand, as he continued to stir, as if he was awakening from a deep sleep. The priest made the sign of the cross, a tear rolled down his face. "Thank you," he said, looking towards Gabriel.

Ethan shook, his head turning from side to side until slowly his eyes opened blinking against the surrounding light. "Momma… Momma don't go," he reached out his hand, weeping. "She was there waiting for me," he said, pointing ahead. "She looked beautiful, no pain, no hurt, she was standing there in the light, all I wanted to do was walk with her, to let go. She to… told me I must come back, I love you Momma."

"Yes Ethan," said Gabriel. "She will await you once again, when you shall walk with all you have loved in this life, for an eternity in the kingdom of God the Father, but you still have work to do here, and you still have a life to live."

"Man, I'm hungry," he said as the twinkle of life sparkled within his large brown eyes. Ben hugged him sobbing. Gabriel smiled down at Ethan who looked upon him wearily, nodding towards him.

They watched as Gabriel moved back against the light. He walked towards where the altar had stood, and slowly rose within the intense glow that poured down like a spiritual shower, his hands outstretched as his outline began to rise beyond the confines of the church, until it disappeared within the brilliance of the serene glow that poured down like a waterfall, until nothing… It was gone.

Father Creegan stumbled forward as he rose to his feet; he sat upon one of the benches that still remained in one piece, looking over towards the detective. No words were needed between the two men as they watched the last strands of light move up against the walls; the priest watched as the oncoming dawn began to filter through the natural darkness of the diminishing nightfall, and he welcomed the new day.

Jack Bannerman walked across towards his sergeant who seemed to be leaning over something. He suddenly stood erect shaking his head.

"Jack, you better take a look at this."

"Take a look at what?" he asked, frowning. Sergeant Foster leaned forward pulling down the hood of one of the dead followers who lay sprawled across the altar's edge, a bloodstained candle stand lay at his side. Bannerman knelt down studying the dead man, it was Chief Superintendent Blake.

"Like he said," replied Bannerman, "evil has many faces, dwelling within many corridors, maybe it's there because we allow it to be, maybe for some their freewill is their burden, and they become a prisoner within their choices."

"What's next Jack?" asked his sergeant. For a moment Bannerman just stared at the crucifix above. "I am going to see my wife," he replied. "She needs me, and I need her." Sergeant Foster just smiled nodding.

In the days to come Monsignor Raffin would call for meetings within the Vatican; these meetings would re-establish our neighbour's bordering lands, where no one creed or culture is signalled out and ostracised, where a common unity is to be found and with one outcome, peace for all man. The process would start slowly, but it was a beginning.

Outside the dawn light spread across the diminishing night. People had gathered in large numbers watching as the last lingering strands of darkness began to shrink across the skyline as if being dragged from the world. It was as if people were in some kind of trance slowly awakening, some just lingered confused, others gathered praying, rejoicing. She had sat by a small fountain, not knowing how she came to be there, she had felt the chill dawn breeze against her skin, blowing through her hair. She had tried to remember but her thoughts were hazy and jumbled. She placed her hands in the cool water, scooping it up as she bathed her face, the water felt cool and refreshing. She turned her hands before her, watching the water drip from her fingers looking upon the smooth skin, slender and perfect; she felt the smooth contours of her face then she remembered.

Sofia Marlow wept, she wept not out of grief as she looked towards the sky. She wept rejoicing, as she had been reborn onto the world.

Yosef Salant watched the sunrise break across the skyline, he watched as it sprayed down upon the ancient tombs upon the Mount of Olives, and he began to pray. He prayed for the souls within them. He prayed for peace in his land, and on this morning as the sun shone as if it was the first sunrise at the beginning of time, he prayed for the grace of God.

THE END

Printed in August 2023
by Rotomail Italia S.p.A., Vignate (MI) - Italy